LAND OF THE
THUNDERING HERDS

LAND OF THE
THUNDERING
HERDS

JUSTIN DENZEL

ILLUSTRATIONS BY
BRENT WATKINSON

PHILOMEL BOOKS ▲ NEW YORK

Land of the Thundering Herds *is set on the prehistoric plains of North America, spanning what are now the states of Kansas, Missouri, Oklahoma and Texas.*

Text copyright© 1993 by Justin Denzel
Illustrations copyright©1993 by Brent Watkinson
Published by Philomel Books, a division of
The Putnam & Grosset Group, 200 Madison Avenue,
New York, NY 10016. All rights reserved.
This book, or parts thereof, may not be reproduced
in any form without permission in writing from the publisher.
Philomel Books, Reg. U.S. Pat. & Tm. Off.
Published simultaneously in Canada.
Book design by Patrick Collins.
The text is set in Aster.

Library of Congress Cataloging-in-Publication Data
Denzel, Justin F.   Land of the thundering herds / Justin Denzel.   p.   cm.
Summary: The adventures and daily routine of a young lion, stallion, condor,
herd of mammoths, and other prehistoric animals sharing a vast grassland.
1. Animals, Fossil—Juvenile fiction. [1. Prehistoric animals—Fiction.] I. Title.
PZ10.3.D415Lan   1993   [Fic]—dc20   92-26222 CIP AC
ISBN 0-399-21894-7

10   9   8   7   6   5   4   3   2   1

First Impression

To Patricia Lee Gauch
with gratitude

▲CONTENTS

LAND OF THE
THUNDERING HERDS

1 ▴ MAMOOT

A WARM SPRING sun beat down on the waves of prairie grass as Mamoot, the old matriarch, guided her family herd of mammoths across the rolling plains. A huge elephantine beast, she stood twelve feet high at the shoulder. Her nimble trunk was constantly in motion, snaking above her head, scratching her ear or throwing dust and straw over her back. As she ambled along she laid her trunk across the old cow in front of her. Then she reached down and stroked Huka, the little calf hobbling along beside her, a gesture of comfort and assurance.

In single file the herd lumbered along. Ba, a big cow, usually took the lead, guided by the rumbling sounds of Mamoot, who trudged along solemnly near the middle. The young juveniles and calves stayed in the center, with another big cow bringing up the rear.

Just out of sight a lone mammoth followed the little herd. He was Taug, Mamoot's son. At fifteen summers, he was nearing maturity. Annoyed by his bumptious and unruly behavior, the big cows had driven him out of the herd. Now, disgruntled and uncertain, he followed at a respectful distance.

The afternoon sun grew warm as Mamoot guided her family toward the swamps and the coolness of the river. Flocks of cowbirds and magpies rode on their broad backs, flying down now and then to feed on the swarms of botflies and grasshoppers stirred up out of the knee-high grass.

Great herds of long-horned bison broke ranks to let the mammoths through. A giant ground sloth, feeding on a plum tree, glanced up, its tiny eyes blinking as it watched the lumbering procession go by. Like golden shadows, bands of pronghorns raced across the plains in front of the mammoths, their white rump patches bobbing in the sunshine.

All at once the wind shifted. Ba stopped and the herd crowded up behind her. Cautious and uncertain, Ba lumbered forward, her head high, her trunk snaking around, testing the air. The rest of the herd stayed back, all gathering about the matriarch, with the calves in the center.

The cowbirds and magpies flew into the air. The bison and horses looked up from their grazing, nostrils flared. Warily they moved away, not in panic but in a slow, deliberate walk. A few of the big bulls turned, their heads low, wide-sweeping horns pointing in the direction of the danger. They stomped their front hooves and bawled noisily.

Filled with curiosity, Huka broke away from the herd and ran up behind Ba. The big cow rumbled deep in her throat. Her ears flicked forward and she stretched out her trunk as she went ahead to investigate. She had gone only a few paces when she threw up her trunk and shook her head, trumpeting loudly. The breeze had picked up and a strong feline scent wafted toward her.

Hidden deep in the yellow grass, two huge saber cats waited, their big amber eyes fastened on Huka.

Brazenly one of the cats came out of cover, her mate still hiding in the tall grass behind her. She walked boldly, in plain sight, directly in front of Ba, challenging her. Ba screamed in anger, her eyes filled with rage. With head high, she charged headlong after the big cat.

Now, for a brief moment, Huka stood alone, unprotected. It was what the male sabertooth was waiting for. He lunged out of the grass, heading directly for the little calf. Huka saw him coming and squealed, rooted to the spot with fear.

The big sabertooth leaped over the ground, his lower jaw hanging open, freeing his fangs for the kill. In another few bounds he would throw himself upon the little calf.

But the old matriarch knew the ruse. Even before the cat sprang out of cover, Mamoot charged ahead. She shoved herself in front of Huka and caught the cat in midair. Savagely she flung him to the ground. Then, with her wide-sweeping tusks, she pressed him against the earth.

The cat struggled and swiped back with his claws. He slashed with his long fangs, but they grazed harmlessly along Mamoot's curved ivory tusks. In a fit of blinding rage the old mammoth knelt on him, cracking his ribs and crushing his skull. With her front feet she stomped the life out of the body. Even after he was dead she continued to vent her anger by dancing around and around on the flattened carcass.

Soon the rest of the herd joined in the ritual of vengeance. Trumpeting and blowing, they trampled the great tawny body into the earth until nothing was left but a wide patch of red-and-yellow fur and a mash of flesh and bones.

Ba came back from her futile chase still blowing and puffing with rage. The other mammoths milled about her, touching her with their trunks, some rubbing against her, assuring her and themselves that everything was all right.

When the excitement passed and the big cows settled down, the herd started out again, heads bobbing, trunks swaying.

Mamoot had fought many saber cats. At fifty-six summers, her brownish-gray skin was scarred and torn and hung on her like a wrinkled leather sack. A scanty growth of hair darkened the ridge of her back and sparsely covered her chin and belly. Her ears were floppy but not large, her long, curving tusks were cracked and stained brown with age.

Now she moved her family along unhurried, heads

swinging, trunks twisting, searching, scratching, grabbing at a clump of pigweed, a tuft of grass, always in motion.

There were six big cows in the little herd other than Mamoot. Three of them were Mamoot's younger sisters; three were her own full-grown offspring. The rest included seven teenagers and two calfs.

Huka jogged along beside the matriarch, sometimes pressing against her, sometimes running between her front legs. She was not his mother but she had been present at his birth, six months ago, and he felt safe and secure with the old cow. From time to time he ran back to his mother to nurse. Then he came back to the matriarch or sauntered up to the front of the column to see what was going on.

Marching across the prairie, their ponderous bodies swayed and jogged in gentle rhythm, covering the ground swiftly in great sweeping strides. The young calves often had to run to keep up.

As she plodded along, Mamoot kept up a constant rumbling sound, talking to Ba, the lead cow, telling her where to turn and when to slow up. At the same time she continued to search the prairie for signs of danger.

Out of the corner of her eye she saw the silent, gray ghosts, the hunting packs of dire wolves loitering around the edges of the grazing bison herds. She paid them little heed, for they were no danger as long as her little family stayed together.

Occasionally she saw a prairie lion slink off through

the yellow grass. They were great, powerful beasts, with long legs for speed and agility. Their sparse manes were light and scraggly. Old Mamoot hated the lions, for although they mostly preyed on the bison, horses and camels, they would not hesitate to pull down an unprotected mammoth calf.

As the herd neared the river, Huka smelled the water. He ran ahead, his little ears flopping up and down, his earlier brush with death completely forgotten.

They made their way along the riverbank, beneath the cool shadows of the cottonwood trees, until they came to the swamp. One by one the huge beasts waded up to their knees in water. They plunged their trunks into the stagnant pools, sucking up the warm water and squirting it into their thirsty mouths.

Huka thrashed about, playfully slapping the water with his trunk then blowing up a huge froth of foam. He chased a frightened heron through the cattails, splashing after it until it flapped into the air and flew away.

After she quenched her thirst, the old matriarch flopped over on her side and covered herself with mud and slime. The thick mud cooled her and she sank down in it and let it penetrate deep into the cracks and crannies of her old body.

Huka lay in the water with only his eyes, the top of his head and his trunk showing. He rested for a moment, closing his eyes, his trunk sticking up like a dead willow branch. Suddenly a large, green dragonfly swooped down, hovered briefly, then landed on the tip of his trunk, its gauzy wings stretched out in the sunlight. The little calf opened one eye as the big insect settled down and began to rub its front legs together. Huka waited quietly. Suddenly, with a loud woosh he snorted, blowing the dragonfly into the water. It floundered about, spinning around on the surface. Then its wings beat a rustling clatter as it lifted itself out of the swamp and flew into the air.

Next Huka climbed over the matriarch's back, slipping and sliding on her wet body. She played with him for a moment, squirting him with mud and water. Then she got up quickly, dumping him into the black ooze. The little calf squealed with delight.

The mud baths over, the matriarch began to feed. As if by signal, the entire herd followed suit. They pulled up tufts of swamp grass with their trunks and slapped them against their front legs to remove the mud before stuffing them into their mouths. Huka tried to imitate them, but his little trunk was not yet strong enough and the wet grass slipped out of his grasp.

Old Mamoot watched him for a moment. Then she snorted and pulled up quads of juicy cattail stalks and stuffed them into the little one's mouth. Huka grunted and swished his tail. He chewed and slobbered noisily as the rich green juices dribbled down his chin.

Not far away Taug, the young bull, waited, keeping the herd just in sight. Up until this spring he had been a part of the little group. Now he was fifteen years old, willful and unruly. So the old cows had driven him out.

But Taug did not understand. Day after day he followed persistently. All his life he had been part of the family. He had grown stronger and heavier than most of the cows, and his tusks jutted out in the great sweeping curves of a mature bull. Now, suddenly, he was an outcast. He loitered along, a little way behind them, resentful and confused, unable to understand this sudden hostility.

He came closer now and saw the calves, the juvenile cows and bulls splashing and playing in the lush swamp grass. Twice within the past few days he had approached the herd, only to be driven off by Ba and the matriarch.

He missed being with them, romping through the shallow water, chasing the younger bulls and cows, touching them in play and tussling with them as he always had. Now, as he stood there, the sharp musky odor of their oozing temporal glands drifted toward him on the warm afternoon breeze. It stirred a strange urge within him and he became restless. He shook his head and lifted his trunk high and decided to try once more to regain his place in the little herd.

Strong and confident, he knew he could dominate most of the cows and his young herd mates. But he was not so sure about Ba and Mamoot. With a deep-throated grumble, he started toward them. As he came closer he held his head high, rising up to his full height.

He lifted his trunk and trumpeted loudly to let them know he was coming.

They turned as a group and came out of the swamp dripping water and mud. There they stood in a little glade surrounded by sandbar willows. They faced him with raised trunks. Not one advanced against him. A feeling of kinship came over him and he almost forgot his anger. They were waiting for him. He saw his young siblings, Tor and Prie, whom he had always played with. He trumpeted again and broke into a run. He was almost upon them now and he felt a warm sense of acceptance.

Just then Ba splashed out of the swamp. She too lifted her head high, her ears spread out, her long, curved tusks confronting him.

Taug stopped short. He saw the anger in her eyes and he knew she had not come to greet him. Once again his temper flared. He walked around her, grumbling in his throat. He snorted and shook his head, swinging his huge, curved tusks, trying to stare her down.

But she did not scare. She came at him with a solid rush. He lowered his head as she crashed into him. Their great tusks clattered and clashed against each other, their heads butted together with a resounding thud. In a fit of rage, Taug wrapped his trunk tightly around hers. He pushed with his massive legs. She dug in her rear legs and pushed back. Locked in this angry embrace they battled, shoving and bellowing.

The rest of the herd stood by. Many of the older cows

ignored the scuffle and went back to their feeding. Mamoot watched with interest, waiting for Ba to drive off the blustering bull.

But Taug had reached maturity. He was bigger than Ba, huskier and stronger. With his trunk twisted around hers he tightened his grip, causing her to grumble in pain. He leaned forward, pushing with his hind legs. She strained against him, but with a mighty lunge he slowly forced her back into the swamp. They splashed and floundered, churning up the muddy waters. Blowing heavily, Ba broke away, shaking her head in anger. She could no longer dominate this young bull. She had helped to raise him, now he had grown beyond her.

Taug splashed out of the water and back onto dry land. He looked around and swept up a trunkful of dust and grass and tossed it over his back in a show of dominance.

Then he heard a deep growling rumble, and he turned to see the matriarch coming toward him. He stood his ground and waited, thinking it was only a bluff. But he was wrong. The big cow bore down on him, her head high, her shrill screech of anger splitting the air. He waited, and a moment later their tusks clashed, throwing him backward almost off his feet. He felt the strength of her superior weight as she slapped him across the face with her trunk and leaned into him.

Taug stumbled backward, reeling before her ponderous attack. He caught himself and heaved against her with all his might, but it was like trying to topple an old burr oak. She did not budge. Instead she smashed back at him with her head. She locked her trunk around his and threw her weight upon him. Taug pushed back. He strained and shoved but this time it was different. He stumbled backward into the swamp, slipping and sliding on the muddy ground. He fell to his knees and for a moment the big cow almost threw him into the water.

Breathing hard, Taug managed to get to his feet as Mamoot whacked him across the shoulder with her tusks and trunk. He looked at her and saw the stubborn fury in her eyes, and he knew his days with the herd were over. He turned quickly and lumbered back across the prairie. The matriarch followed, flaying him with her trunk. With his head down he continued on, far across the plains, and the old matriarch let him go.

That night Taug wandered alone across the prairie. A big yellow moon hung in the sky and he heard the coughing roar of the prairie lions. Crickets sang in the tall grass and dire wolves howled in the distance. Taug was lonely but not afraid. He was a prairie giant and nothing could touch him. He would travel far and find other bulls of his own age. But he would never come back to the herd of his mother.

The old matriarch returned to her family, the incident already forgotten. Taug was not the first son she had driven from the herd. But he was the last.

2 ▲ TERATORN

TERATORN CIRCLED IN the brazen sky as he soared on silent wings high over the rolling plains. He was hungry and his ominous shadow brought fear and panic to the small creatures on the grasslands below. Nervous prairie dogs yapped and barked, then scurried for the safety of their burrows. Young deer fawns stayed close to their mothers.

For one brief moment the dark shadow touched a covey of quail. Instantly the frightened birds exploded into the air rather than be caught huddled on the ground. Teratorn circled again, then swooped down, gliding over the shallow pan lake where hundreds of teal and mallards rose into the air in panic, a living wave of roaring, beating wings.

A giant beaver looked up from its grubbing around the roots of a sandbar willow as the massive flock of frightened mallards flew close overhead. He blinked his dark, beady eyes, then turned back to his digging.

A huge stag moose waded knee-deep in the shallows, feeding on the raft of water lilies. He didn't even bother to look up, for he, like the giant beaver, had no fear of Teratorn.

Yet there were many that trembled under the shadow of the great wings, many like the storks and gangly herons that speared for leopard frogs and water snakes along the edges of the prairie lakes and ponds; many like the plovers and turkeys that stalked through the short grass or the jackrabbits that ran zigzag paths across it. To them Teratorn's shadow meant death, and they fled in terror before it. He was the scourge of their lives. He was the giant prehistoric hunting condor of the great plains. Twice the size of an ordinary condor, he searched the prairie for the carcass of a dead bison or mammoth. Yet with his huge, hooked bill he could hunt like an eagle. So a pronghorn kid or a lost lion cub would serve as well.

Teratorn turned his naked, orange-and-yellow head from side to side, searching. He circled again, then picked up a thermal, a warm column of air rising from the prairie. On outstretched wings he sailed within the tepid updraft, feeling its lift carry him higher and higher. With a fourteen-foot wingspread and primary feathers deeply slotted, he could soar for hours, covering vast distances over this sea of grass.

When sailing effortlessly in a cloud-flecked sky he was graceful and majestic. On the ground he waddled about with wings half closed, grim-faced and clumsy.

This morning Teratorn soared lazily, circling, gliding from one thermal to the next, his vast domain spread out below him. With sharp telescopic vision he surveyed the endless plains. He followed the meandering rivers, marked by wide green borders of swamp oak and cottonwoods. He saw the shallow pan lakes, flashing in the sun like so many glittering mirrors. He stretched out his wings and let the warm updraft carry him higher until he could make out the towering escarpments of red sandstone far off to the west.

Below him, Teratorn could see the teeming herds of long-horned bison grazing peacefully on the waving fields of grama grass. They wandered in close-packed throngs or in long, staggering columns up and down the prairie hills and along the shallow valleys from one end of the horizon to the other.

Here and there family herds of gigantic mammoths and bands of horses intermingled with the bison—all grazing side by side with elk, pronghorn antelopes and camels.

Teratorn banked and glided lower. His keen eyes picked up a flat-headed peccary sow and her litter of piglets. Out in the open, away from the protective shelter of the river shrubs, they rooted for grubs in a field of buffalo grass. The big condor folded his wings and plummeted down. His aim was good but his shadow swept the ground before him, passing over the feeding pigs. Instantly the sow squealed and raced for the nearby thickets. The litter followed quickly. But one of the piglets tarried too long. Teratorn swooped down and snatched it up in his bill. He carried it into the branches of a cottonwood tree. The tiny pig was hardly more than a mouthful. It kicked and squirmed. The big condor slapped it against the branch, ending its life. Then he threw back his head and swallowed it whole.

After he had rested, Teratorn hopped off his perch. He caught a sweeping updraft and let it carry him high into the air. Sailing in a wide arch, he searched the prairie and the meandering river. Off on the far horizon he saw a flight of circling vultures. He tilted his wings and began his glide, heading directly for the gathering of soaring birds. The wind whispered through his pinions and he dropped swiftly. Down, down he went as the grasslands and trees rushed up to meet him.

Just below him a great brown body lay stretched out on the yellow grass. It was a freshly killed giant ground sloth. A pair of huge sabertooth cats were feeding on it. In a dead burr oak a short distance away a group of vultures sat brooding, waiting their turn at the feast.

Without hesitation Teratorn swooped to the ground. He hunched low and looked around, then hopped forward like an ungainly kangaroo. Cautiously he waddled closer to the dead beast. One of the big cats looked up and growled. Two long saber fangs hung down from its upper jaw and blood dripped from its flat snout.

Teratorn opened his wings and backed away. But both cats were gorged with fresh meat and were ready to leave the carcass. With full bellies and a parting snarl, they slunk off to the shade of the distant cotton-wood trees to sleep and digest their meal.

In an awkward shuffle, Teratorn approached the carcass. He hopped up on the dead sloth and began to eat, thrusting his naked head into the open gut where the big cats had been feeding.

One by one the hungry vultures flapped out of the burr oak. They waddled up to the kill, thrusting out their long, naked heads, trying to snatch a scrap of meat. Teratorn glared at them and hissed. Like hunched-back mourners, they fell back, hissing in return, waiting for their turn at the carcass.

Far off, on a hillside overlooking the prairie, a pack of dire wolves had also seen the big vultures circling. They watched as one by one the big birds dropped out of the sky. They knew it meant food, and now in long, steady strides they hurried toward the scene.

Teratorn ate quickly, swallowing huge chunks of meat in massive gulps. He had not been eating long when the hungry pack of dire wolves arrived. They snarled and snapped at him, driving him off the carcass. Had it been only one or two wolves Teratorn might have fought them off, but a pack of nine was more than he could handle. Reluctantly he backed away from the kill, hissing in protest. The big wolves tore into the dead beast, fighting among themselves as Teratorn and the vultures looked on.

For a while Teratorn slouched back and forth impatiently. Then he could wait no longer. His appetite still not satisfied, he faced into the breeze, opened his wings and ran across the grassland. Within a short distance he felt the lift under his wings. Once in the air he circled into the wind, soaring upward into the prairie sky.

Again he followed the winding river, fringed with the green of the cottonwood trees. He searched closely as the golden prairie swept away beneath him. His keen eyes played over the land, looking for a grubbing marmot or a prairie dog too far from its burrow.

Then, on the near side of a hill he saw three gray dots scrambling and tumbling in the bunchgrass below. Quickly he circled lower. They were dire wolf pups playing away from their den. Teratorn closed his wings and started down with the bright sun behind him. He came like a meteorite on muffled pinions.

Unaware of the danger, the three pups wrestled and tumbled in the dry grass as Teratorn plummeted. No warning scream, no hiss escaped his lips. In complete silence he slashed the nearest pup with his hammerlike talon, breaking its back as he swooped past. The second pup he caught in his bill, carrying it by the nape of its neck, shaking it violently. It was dead in an instant. The third pup yelped in panic and raced for the safety of the den.

Teratorn closed his wings and landed, hopping clumsily across the ground. He glanced around cautiously, jerking his head from side to side. The bright orange-and-yellow skin of his naked skull and neck flashed in the sunlight. Without waiting, he threw back his head and swallowed the pup whole. After a few gulps to get it down, he waddled over to the pup with the broken back. It was limp and lifeless. He picked it up in his great bill, threw back his head again and swallowed. While the dire wolves were dining on the fallen ground sloth, Teratorn was eating their pups.

The big condor stood there for a moment, waiting for the meal to reach his crop. Then he opened his wings, faced into the breeze and began running. He was heavier now and it took longer for the wind to give him lift. But before many steps he flapped clumsily into the air. A moment later he caught an updraft coming off the hill. He stretched his wings out to their full length and soared effortlessly into the sky. Twice he circled, then headed directly for the escarpment forty miles away.

High on one of the lofty pinnacles he found his nest. With half-closed wings he slowed his ascent and landed lightly beside his mate. He hunched forward and retched, disgorging his partially digested meal onto the bare rock. A young chick, already larger than an eagle, came out from under the female's wings. It fell upon the partly digested meat, gulping it down greedily. What little was left went to the female.

Soon a bright red sun sank slowly behind the escarpment. Teratorn fluffed up his feathers and tucked his bare head under his wing. It was time to sleep. Tomorrow he would hunt again.

3 ▲ EQUUS

EARLY-MORNING SUN FILTERED through the leaves of the lone burr oak. It was the first light Equus had ever seen, the beginning of true awareness. He had just come from within the darkness of his mother's womb, and now he lay in the shadowed prairie grass, staring through the wet, lucent membrane of the fetal sack.

The mare was already on her feet, nosing her new-born foal, smelling it, prodding it to life. Kang, the big herd stallion, pranced nervously, tossing his head and nickering as he circled around his small band of mares and yearlings.

They were large, dun-colored animals with dark, bristling manes running down the napes of their necks. Wary and tough, they roamed the plains in small family groups, intermingling freely with the wandering herds of bison and pronghorns.

Stimulated by the light, Equus moved for the first time, stretching, puncturing the fetal sack with his tiny hooves. Thick, watery fluid poured out, trickling between the stalks of dry prairie grass. The mare reached down and licked him around the mouth and neck and on the abdomen.

For a few moments the little foal lay still, breathing heavily. Then he kicked and struggled and tried to stand on thin, unsteady legs. The birth membrane slid off. The umbilical cord severed and Equus was free, a living, breathing part of this golden prairie. He sank down again, his legs folded beneath him, his head wobbling, large brown eyes staring out at this strange new world.

Before long the little colt struggled to his feet, his legs splayed out, still shaky and unsteady. He lifted his head and looked at his mother. Their damp noses met, imprinting their distinctive odors on each other's brain.

Kang continued pacing in wide circles, herding his little band close, at the same time watching for the gray ghosts of dire wolves or the tawny shadow of a prairie lion. All that afternoon he waited nervously while the newborn foal gained strength.

Soon Equus found his mother's teats and suckled as she stood quietly, letting him drink long and full. When he had finished he settled down beside her, his legs tucked up beneath him while she groomed and licked him from head to tail until his light brown coat was shiny and soft.

He had large, lustrous eyes. His head was shapely,

with well-formed ears and a dark, stiff mane standing up along the nape of his neck.

Around the two, the other horses grazed quietly, seemingly unconcerned. All except one grizzled old mare, who stood off to one side watching intently. She had not had a foal in many summers and the newborn colt excited her. She stretched out her neck and ambled toward it, sniffing.

The young mother swung around and nickered softly in protest, telling the old one to stay away.

But the old mare ignored the warning. Aroused by her maternal instincts, she sauntered closer.

Equus scrambled to his feet and backed away in fright. His mother whinnied, her eyes rolling up in a wild look. She stretched out her neck, pulling back her upper lip as she bared her teeth.

Still the old one came on.

The young mare whinnied. She reared up on her hind legs, pawing, striking out with her sharp hooves. The grizzled one backed away, but only for a moment. Brazenly she pranced around and came in from the opposite side. Once again the young mother drove her off. She chased after the old one, squealing in anger, nipping at her with steel-hard teeth.

Alerted by the cries and pounding hooves, Kang galloped in to break up the fight. He separated the two mares, then butted the old one with his head, sending her off across the prairie. She pranced away but stopped for a moment to lick her left front leg, where the sharp hoof of the young mother had opened a slight cut just above the tendon. Then she limped away and calmly joined the other horses grazing along the bottom of the hill.

Within four days Equus was able to keep up with the others. His mother's milk was rich in protein and he grew strong and sturdy. Spirited and full of life, he ran on long, spindly legs, galloping over the prairie, racing in and around the band of horses, up and down the hills. Exploding with energy, he pranced and jumped in wild, buoyant moods. He chased big swallowtails and raced after bounding jackrabbits. Yet he was careful not to stray too far from his mother.

Kang moved his mares and colts along slowly from day to day, watching over them closely as they grazed. He guided them between the straggling herds of bison, signaling his lead mare by a head toss, a flick of the ear or a nicker.

One afternoon he took them down to the pan lake. He stopped on top of a steep rise overlooking the water. There he glanced around guardedly, testing the air. His keen nostrils detected no danger.

The lake was peaceful and quiet. Along the shoreline hundreds of mallards and pintails paddled about in loose rafts, feeding in and around the arrowheads and pickerelweeds. Here and there tall white storks waded patiently in the shallows, spearing for frogs and minnows.

Satisfied that the way was clear, Kang walked down

to the edge of the lake. He paced back and forth for a moment, glancing around, sniffing. Then he nickered softly. Immediately the entire band came trotting down to the water.

A stately blue heron moved aside as the horses gathered in a row along the edge of the lake. Equus followed his mother's example, reaching down, pursing his lips and drawing up the clear liquid. He stared into the water as he drank long and deep. Once he jumped back, startled as a school of killifish darted under his nose.

Soon large herds of long-horned bison came down to the pan to drink. They bawled and shoved, jostling for space at the water's edge. Groups of pronghorn antelopes arrived, with kids by their sides, always skittish, ready to take flight.

The sun was warm and the soft hum of bumblebees around the blue flags added a melodic note.

Suddenly, all around the pan, heads went up. Streams of water dripped from muzzles. Equus turned, following the gaze of his mother as Mamoot and her family came down the hill to the edge of the water.

The horses hurriedly stole another drink, then quietly turned and stepped aside as the mammoths lumbered into the water.

Kang moved his band into the high grass on the side of the hill. Some of the mares browsed on the new green shoots of pigweed, others rolled on the ground, scratching their backs in the dry grass.

Filled with curiosity, Equus watched the huge mammoths as they plunged their long trunks into the lake and sprayed water over their broad backs, chasing the attendant cowbirds into the air. He was used to the giant ground sloths and he had walked beside the big longhorns. But these ponderous beasts were even larger.

Just then Huka came splashing out of the pond. Equus stared in wonder at the little mammoth. He watched intently as Huka hobbled along the shore, swinging his trunk about with great energy, shaking the water from his back.

All at once Huka spied Equus. He turned quickly and reached out his trunk.

Equus whinnied and tossed his head as the mammoth calf came toward him. He waited, then stepped back, curious but unsure. Slowly, one step at a time, Huka continued to advance, holding his trunk straight out in front of him.

Equus stamped his hoof. Huka stopped and tilted his head to one side. He made a soft swishing sound, then came on again.

This time Equus turned and ran. He galloped up the hill, through the tall grass. When he reached the top he turned to see Huka hobbling along close behind him, his ears flopping, his trunk swinging. Realizing that it was a game, Equus galloped back down the hill. Huka saw him coming. He turned quickly and started to run in the opposite direction, with the little colt following.

They galloped around through the tall grass, in and out between the herds of horses and pronghorns and down along the shore of the lake. They chased each other back and forth, first one taking the lead then the other.

The mammoths went on with their bathing, the horses grazed peacefully as the little colt and the mammoth galloped in and around them.

All at once Huka stopped and Equus caught up to him. The little mammoth reached out his trunk. Equus stretched out his neck. For one brief moment their noses touched.

During it all, Kang stood on the top of the hill overlooking the pan lake. With a wary eye he kept guard, searching the prairie as far as he could see. His eyes were sharp, his nose was keen. He could smell danger from far away and now a deep, pungent odor made his nostrils flare. It was the smell of cat. Kang stomped his front hoof and whinnied. Immediately the horses stopped their grazing. Equus broke off his game and galloped up to his mother.

All around the pan lake the bison lifted their heads. They splashed out of the water, grunting and blowing. They moved off to the west, followed by groups of pronghorns and scattered bands of horses. They walked slowly at first, then gradually broke into a trot as the sound of their running thundered across the plains.

Kang rounded up his band. This time he took the

lead and guided it out across the prairie at a brisk canter. Equus ran along beside his mother. The grizzled old mare followed close behind.

Soon two male prairie lions came out of the tall grass. Heavy muscles rippled under their massive shoulders as they crept down toward the pan lake. When they saw the mammoths they stopped and crouched down, waiting.

Unlike the horses and bison, the mammoths had no horrifying fear of the big cats. As if to assert their dominance they lingered for one last drink. Then Mamoot rumbled in her throat, and with leisurely strides the little herd ambled off, heading for the stand of cottonwood trees on the distant horizon.

As soon as the mammoths left, the big lions went down to the edge of the lake. Their great shaggy heads rested on massive paws as they hunched down, side by side, and lapped at the water. When they were finished drinking they licked their black lips with long, pink tongues. They stood up and looked around for a moment. Then they turned and loped out across the prairie in steady pursuit of the fleeing herds of bison and horses.

4 ▲ PANTHERA

PANTHERA LAY IN the tall meadow grass, blending in with the tawny hues of the rolling prairie. She could hear the pounding thunder of the hooves coming from the direction of the pan lake. Expectantly she gathered her legs beneath her, ready to spring. She was a giant prairie lion, powerful, eleven feet in length and more than four feet high at the shoulder. Her legs were long and lanky like a cheetah's, and for short distances she could run faster than her prey. But she had to get in close to begin her charge. She waited now, tensely, as the stampede came on.

The rumbling sounds of the stampede came closer and closer until the earth trembled beneath her. She felt it throb and vibrate in her bones and against her chest pressed hard against the earth. She waited, her muscles taut, jet-black pupils staring out of amber eyes. Soon she could see the yellow cloud of dust rolling toward her and out of it the roaring, thundering herd.

Thousands of long-horned bison led the way, huge cows, bawling calves and massive bulls with shaggy manes and great wide-sweeping horns. They galloped past her, rushing on headlong, grunting, snorting, wind rasping in their throats. Bands of pronghorn antelopes and horses mingled with them, all pounding hard, their dark eyes flashing panic. The flying hooves and slashing horns were fraught with danger. But Panthera had cubs to feed. Instinct and a growling stomach told her it was time to hunt. She moved cautiously, creeping forward slowly as the galloping hordes came on. The mixed herds passed in a crushing mass of thundering hooves that stretched across the plains. Carefully she scanned the fleeing beasts, searching for an easy victim.

A sudden breeze passed through the crowd of panicky bison. Panthera could smell the acrid odor of their bodies. Then another smell drifted toward her on the wind. She twitched her nose and could almost pinpoint its source. It was the two male lions of her pride coming down from the pan lake. The feline odor of their tawny bodies urged the herds along, quickening the stampede.

Across the prairie from Panthera, four other female lions waited in ambush. Two of them were her sisters, the other two her full-grown daughters. Hunched down in the tall grass, they too watched patiently to single out a kill.

Panthera edged closer, her eyes staring, studying each passing wave, searching for a likely victim. She would not charge into the mass of pounding hooves, where she might be trampled. Rather she watched for stragglers along the edges, a lagging calf, an infirm bull. From long experience she could quickly pick out the weak, the sick and the infirm.

She inched forward again, her tail switching with pent-up tension. Her ears lay back, her muscles quivered, her pink tongue flicked out and licked her jowls.

The sound of the thundering hooves was deafening now. It seemed to come from all directions. Clouds of dust rose up, obscuring Panthera's vision. She saw the tawny flashes of speeding antelopes, the sweep of heavy shoulders and massive horns of the bison. Each time she killed a large animal she was risking her own life. Now, in this mad flight of panic, the prairie was alive with danger.

Panthera blinked, uncertain. The press of bodies, the noise and boiling dust distracted her attention. She waited, staring intently at the wild confusion.

Grunting, heads bobbing, the fleeing herds passed in wave after wave. Then Panthera's body stiffened. She saw Kang and his band of horses galloping down along the outside of the surging herds. Her eyes fastened on Equus, racing along beside his mother. The young colt's hooves flew over the ground. But he grew tired, and little by little he fell back. His mother slowed her pace to stay with him. Except for the grizzled old mare trailing along just behind them, they were the last of the band.

Panthera pushed herself to her feet and started forward, sliding along through the grass one step at a time as the mother and colt came closer. Then she stopped and gauged the distance carefully. Suddenly, with a bounding leap, she exploded out of the tall grass, her lithe body flying across the ground. The mare saw her coming. With a quick change of stride she swerved, placing herself between Equus and Panthera. But now she had nowhere to turn. She could only drive ahead on the same course, hoping to outrun the charging lioness.

It was a mistake. Instantly Panthera sensed the advantage. She leaped over the ground, closing the distance. She knew the colt's lack of speed was holding up the mare. If she could bring down the mother, the colt would linger nearby, an easy kill for one of the other lions.

With a renewed rush, Panthera surged ahead, her long, powerful legs driving her over the ground. Out of the corner of her eye she saw the mare galloping hard, her nostrils flaring, her tail flying out behind her. The gap was closing fast. A few more bounds and their paths would converge.

Then suddenly through the haze of churning dust Panthera saw the grizzled old mare galloping along behind the colt. Quickly the lioness's keen eyes detected the slight limp, the momentary hesitation in gait, the unmistakable sign of infirmity. In that instant Panthera turned.

The grizzled old mare saw the lioness change course.

Her ears went back and her eyes rolled up in her head in stark terror. For twenty summers she had chased the wind. She had galloped across the plains, roaming the prairies with the little band. She had raised her foals. Now she was old. Her bones were stiff and tired. The slight injury to her front leg made the difference. In a last, desperate move she lunged toward the herd of stampeding bison to lose herself in the crush of bodies. But it was too late.

With a wild leap the lioness pounced, grabbing the old mare around the haunches, clawing her, throwing her to the ground. Quickly the old mare got to her feet. Panthera spun around and reached again. Once more the sharp claws dug into the mare's rump in an attempt to pull her down. The mare strained hard, hind legs thrashing, dragging the lioness with her. Panthera's claws dug deeper. Red welts of blood slashed across the mare's hide as Panthera slowly began to slide off. An instant later she let go. At the same time she felt a blinding flash of pain as the mare's left rear hoof flew up and cracked her solidly beneath the lower jaw.

Stunned by the sudden blow, Panthera tumbled over the ground. When she stopped rolling she lay in the grass, blood trickling from the corner of her mouth. Through a blur of vision she watched as two of her sisters pulled down the old mare. One grabbed her under the throat, crushing her windpipe. The other clamped her jaws over the mare's muzzle, cutting off her air.

With a heavy groan the mare tried to get up but the lions held fast, pinning her to the ground. For a few moments the old mare squirmed and kicked. Her chest heaved, wheezing for air. Soon her struggles grew weak then ceased altogether. Her eyes rolled up into her head. Her legs stretched out and she kicked feebly for the last time. The stampede passed on around her.

Panthera lay there, watching it all, unable to help. Her lower jaw was half open, already rigid, the throbbing pain pounded in her head.

The thundering sounds of the stampede faded into the distance as the two male lions arrived to take over the kill. The lionesses snarled, but the big males chased them off with savage growls. The females waited nearby while the males tore at the dead mare. Snarling and fighting, they opened the soft underbelly with sharp fangs and claws and began feeding greedily on the soft belly meat. With slobbering grunts they gobbled down huge chunks of the inner thighs. When they were finished they walked off slowly toward the river and the shade of the big cottonwood trees, their bloated bellies hanging full.

Now it was the females' turn to feed. Side by side they tore and pulled at the carcass. They ate quietly, more tolerant of each other's company than the males. Panthera crouched beside them, licking at the bloodied carcass. Her jaw was stiff, her left eye was swollen almost shut, a dull throbbing ache racked her brain.

Unable to eat, Panthera got up and made her way

through the stand of cottonwoods. She passed the sleeping males, lying in the shade, one on his back, all four legs curled up into the air, the other beast lazily draped over the fallen limb of a willow tree.

Panthera walked by without stopping and went directly toward a thicket of buckthorns, where her cubs were waiting. Metan, the bold one, came out to meet her. His brother, more timid, waited in the shadows. Out of a litter of four, they were the last to survive.

Metan hobbled up to his mother. He pressed his cheek along her neck and shoulder. Unaware of her injury, he licked the dried blood from around her lips. The second cub ran up, mewing softly. Panthera nudged them with the side of her head, then led them up to the carcass.

Bold and unruly, Metan ran ahead. He snarled and spit at the vultures already gathering a few yards away from the kill. They backed away and glared down at him with savage stares.

Even at this early age Metan was reckless and aggressive. Normally his carelessness would have marked him for death. But there was something different about the bold one. Maybe it was an additional thimbleful of gray matter in his brain, a tenth degree more intelligence. He possessed a streak of independence and daring not given to the others.

One of Panthera's sisters was already at the kill with her three cubs. Without waiting, Metan shouldered his way between them. With sharp teeth he tugged and pulled at the soft belly meat, tearing it into bite-size strips. Pools of partially congealed blood collected in the bottom of the upturned rib cage. Greedily Metan lapped them up and ran his small, pink tongue around his lips, looking for more.

The vultures pressed closer around the carcass, impatient to get at the kill.

Panthera waited nearby, hungry but unable to feed because of her swollen jaw. She flicked her ears and shook her head as blowflies and hornets buzzed around her lips, attracted by the oozing blood.

When her cubs finished feeding, Panthera led them back to the river and the safety of the elder thickets. There, with pain still throbbing in her head, she turned over on her side in a patch of the soft moss and let them nurse.

As the days passed Panthera grew weaker. Unable to hunt or feed, she lost weight. Her ribs began to show. She lay in the shade of the buckthorn bushes with her eyes closed, breathing heavily. Botflies circled her head, laying eggs in her nostrils and in the corners of her blood-encrusted lips.

Metan and his brother grew weak. They walked about on unsteady legs, mewing and crying. Many times they tried to nurse but, without nourishment, Panthera's milk dried up. Metan rubbed against her feverish body, urging her to let him nurse. But she lay still and did not open her eyes. He tugged at her ear and pawed at the end of her tail. It no longer slapped back in play.

Metan's round belly became bloated with gas. Hungry and restless, he left his brother and went down to the river. He crouched on the edge of the bank and lapped at the water. Damselflies fluttered among the blue flags. A pair of pintails flew up and disappeared into the reeds.

Metan looked around, searching for something to eat. Then suddenly a fat brown toad the size of his paw hopped under his nose. Instinctively he pounced on it, holding it close between his paws. The toad closed its eyes and puffed up its body. Metan held fast. He clamped his jaws over it and began to chew. Instantly a white, viscous fluid seeped from around the toad's head. Metan tasted it then jumped back, releasing his hold. He felt a sharp, stinging sensation on his tongue. It spread quickly inside his cheeks and over the roof of his mouth. It burned his throat. He shook his head vigorously. Flecks of white froth flew from his lips. Furiously he began lapping at the water to cool his tongue.

Only slightly injured, the toad hopped away. Metan let it go. He wanted no more of it.

Still hungry, he went up the low embankment then through a stand of sumacs to the edge of the thicket. There he met his brother, mewing and crying. Together they crept out onto the prairie, searching for something to eat.

As they pushed through the yellow grass a covey of quail flushed in front of them. Metan jumped quickly but missed as the birds flew out of reach. Next he chased a colored lizard into a rocky outcrop. He pawed at the crevasse where the lizard had disappeared. He sniffed and scratched and peered into the dark slit. The lizard was gone.

Recklessly Metan led the way out onto the open grassland, where they found a bumbling box turtle. Metan stalked it and slapped it with his paw each time it came out of its shell. He rolled it over and tried to bite it, but his small teeth made little impression.

He was lying there, waiting for it to come out again when a dark shadow swept across the ground in front of him. He glanced up quickly and saw Teratorn swooping out of the sky directly toward him. For an instant Metan stood fast, as though rooted to the spot. Then, just as the shadow was about to engulf him, he leaped to one side and pressed himself flat into the grass. He felt the gust of wind and heard the clicking sound of the savage beak as the huge wings passed close overhead.

As soon as the big condor flew by, Metan jumped up and raced for the nearby trees. When he reached the safety of the thickets he glanced back to see his brother following close behind. But the little cub had waited too long. The giant condor swooped around and snatched him up in his great beak. The last thing Metan saw was his brother kicking and squirming as he was carried off in Teratorn's bill.

Hungry and uncertain, Metan wandered back into the buckthorn bushes. There his mother was still lying in the shadows. He crouched down beside her for a while, tired and half asleep. Then he rolled over and pushed his snout into her abdomen and tried to nurse. Her belly was cold and as stiff as dried oak bark. Metan got up and sniffed around her. He touched her shoulder with his paw. She did not move. Her eyes were half closed, cold and glassy.

5 ▲ GUNDAR

THAT NIGHT MAMOOT kept her family of mammoths down near the swamps. The next morning, after the sun cleared away the early mists, she guided them out across the prairie. They grazed leisurely, without hurry, shuffling and swaying as they ambled along.

Huka stayed close to the matriarch. He watched her reach down with her trunk and curl it around a clump of grass. She pulled it taut, then kicked it with her right front foot, cutting it off just above the roots with her sharp nails. Huka waited, then lifted his trunk, begging. The old cow grunted and flapped her ears. She rolled up a bunch of grass and stuffed it into his mouth.

Around midday the old matriarch stopped feeding. Her trunk went up, sniffing the air. She rumbled deep in her throat and turned, staring off into the distance. Ba and the other big cows turned with her. They sniffed and rubbed against each other in a flurry of excitement.

The calves squealed and Huka ran about in circles, his floppy ears bouncing up and down.

The little family crowded together, all eyes staring toward the distant river. Mamoot continued her low rumbling calls, at the same time scooping up trunkfuls of dust and grass and tossing them over her back.

Huka's small body trembled with anticipation as he waited impatiently.

Then, from out of the stand of far-off cottonwood trees, came a horde of giant shadows, more mammoths, a great herd of them. With heads held high and trunks swaying, they approached the little group. There were more than one hundred of them, full-grown cows each with great curving tusks, accompanied by immature cows and bulls and many calves. Some of the cows were even larger than Mamoot. Amid loud trumpeting calls, deep rumblings and high-pitched squeals the herds met and mingled. It was the meeting of the clans, a gathering of kinship groups that went back for hundreds of years.

The big cows greeted each other with elaborate displays of affection, clanking their tusks together, rubbing against each other, embracing and intertwining their trunks.

Huka gamboled about among the milling beasts, tugging and tussling with the other calves, butting heads with them. The big cows hugged him and caressed him with their trunks. He brushed against them and felt the throbbing vibrations of their bodies. He smelled them and put the tip of his trunk into their mouths. Many of them were his distant aunts and cousins, his kith and kin. Within a few weeks they would leave, to go their separate ways, and he might not see them again for another year.

As the day passed, more family groups began to come until the plains were crowded with the massive beasts. But it was spring and the prairie was lush with new grass. There was ample grazing for all, and the time was ripe for procreation.

Many of the young cows were ready for new calves and Ba was one of them. Powerful secretions flowed through her body. Her cheek glands seeped with dark, viscous fluids and she felt a persistent urge. She had had her last calf more than four summers ago. Now she wanted another. Deep in her massive chest she began to sing. It was a heavy, throbbing song, an ultra-low rumble that carried out over the prairie like an inaudible message, meant only for the ears of her own kind. It was a love song. The bison, grazing only a short distance away, never heard it. The pronghorns and the horses were deaf to its call.

But there was one who did hear it, a giant bull far out of sight, feeding deep in the swamp beyond the bend of the river. Fourteen feet tall at the shoulder, he stood as high as the sumac trees, and he had a spread of great curving tusks. He was Gundar the patriarch. Ornery and short-tempered, his huge body was temporarily gripped in a torment of "musth," a frenzied, physical condition that came over him more and more as he grew older. He reeked with strong earthy odors that came from every part of his body, and his cheeks were stained dark with patches of thick, oily fluids oozing from his temporal glands. A small flock of cowbirds rode on his back and shoulders, feeding on the ticks and leeches that lived in the cracks of his ancient hide.

Gundar heard the throbbing love call. He lifted his trunk and tested the air. Then grunting and rumbling he splashed out of the swamp, leaving a trail of dripping water. He walked across the prairie in great lumbering strides, his body swaying, his head swinging. The grazing herds of bison and camels quietly moved aside to let him pass.

When he reached the matriarch's herd, Ba was standing off to one side with three bulls around her. Two of them were young, not fully grown. But the third one was Big Bull, a huge old patriarch like Gundar.

Anger blazed in Gundar's eyes. Almost twice their size, he turned on the two young bulls. He lifted his head high, displaying his wide-sweeping tusks. One of the bulls backed away, bowing and nodding in submission. But the other one stood his ground.

Grumbling loudly, Gundar charged. He plowed into the brash youngster and easily bowled him over. Quickly the young bull lifted himself to his feet. But Gundar was upon him, slapping him with his trunk, forcing him back until the young bull's legs buckled and he fell to his knees. He got up again, grunting and puffing, but he had had enough. The old giant was far too strong for him. He turned quickly and followed the first bull off across the prairie.

Gundar was not even breathing hard as he turned to face Big Bull. Like Gundar, the old patriarch was scarred and ear-torn from many battles. Now both bulls lifted their heads high and measured their tusks.

Gundar snorted as if in contempt. He swung his trunk across the ground, blowing up dust. Big Bull stood firm, glaring. Gundar flapped his ears, wafting some of the strong odor from his temporal glands toward the old patriarch. Big Bull advanced boldly, kicking up clouds of dust.

For a few moments the two giants circled slowly, grumbling and staring at each other. Gundar pulled up a red cedar bush, roots and all. He slapped it against his leg, then smashed it to the ground, venting his temper.

Big Bull bellowed and swung his long, curved tusks through the tall grass. For a long moment they stood there eyeing each other. Neither would back down.

Then suddenly Big Bull lunged. Gundar met him head on with a resounding clash of ivory tusks. Gundar wrapped his trunk around Big Bull's and held on tight. He dug in his hind legs and pushed. Big Bull shoved back. Like two unmovable boulders, they heaved against each other.

The matriarch and her family paid little attention to the fight. They went on grazing a short distance away.

All except Huka, who pressed against Mamoot, his eyes wide with wonder as he watched the brawling battle.

Snorting and blowing, the two bulls separated. They backed away momentarily, only to charge once more. The sound of the battle echoed over the prairie as they clashed again and again. With trunks entwined, they strained against each other, tearing up the earth, trampling a wide circle in the tall grass. Their inward-curving tusks acted as shields, usually preventing serious injury, making it a battle of strength and endurance.

Gundar tightened his grip around Big Bull's trunk. But Big Bull spread out his pillar-like legs and refused to be thrown off balance. They were breathing heavily now, blowing and snorting, the air wheezing in their throats. Gundar's face was wet as the oozing secretions from his temporal glands dripped down the side. Twice he stumbled, almost going to his knees. The fight dragged on, and he felt the strength draining out of him.

In frustrated rage Big Bull coiled his trunk up under his chin and charged in like a ram. Gundar was waiting for him, and their heads smashed together with a resounding thud. Stunned and shaken, Gundar stood there as if in a trance, weaving back and forth. Without waiting, Big Bull crashed into him again and Gundar fell to his knees. Now Big Bull saw his chance. He wrapped his trunk around Gundar's head and pulled mightily in an effort to topple the tired giant. But his trunk slipped off the wet hide. Momentum hurled him forward and he stumbled and fell to the ground and rolled over on his side.

By now Gundar was fully awake and on his feet. He rushed at the fallen mammoth, lashing out at him, grazing him with his tusks, leaving a shallow scar across his tough hide. Each time Big Bull tried to get up, Gundar pushed him to the ground.

The sun was down now and the first shadows of darkness fell over the plains.

Now, weary of the fight, Gundar stepped back and let the old bull get up. Big Bull stood for a moment, reeling from side to side. His head was low and he wheezed badly.

Gundar waited, uncertain, almost ready to give up. Then he watched with surprise as Big Bull turned and staggered off into the gathering gloom.

Gundar let him go. He gave no trumpeting call, no sign of victory. He was too tired and worn.

For three days he remained with Mamoot's family. He had sired many of their calves. Now he would father another. He stayed next to Ba, never leaving her side. During that time they mated.

A few days later Gundar wandered off to live again as a nomad, until another love call came his way. In the meantime Ba carried the seed of a new life deep in her womb. Within two years she would give birth to another calf.

6 ▲ METAN

FOR TWO DAYS Metan lingered under the shadows of the buckthorn bushes, near the dead body of his mother. He mewed plaintively and rubbed his cheek against her stiff, cold muzzle. Baffled and uncertain, he kept coming back, stroking her with his paw, unable to understand why she did not get up.

Soon the relentless goad of hunger drove him away. He turned and padded off through the cottonwood trees and down to the river. Black-and-white magpies scolded from the branches of the coralberry bushes. A brown toad plopped across his path. Recent memory stirred and he backed away. Hungry as he was, he would not touch it.

He heard the low *chuck-chuck* cry of rails feeding in the reeds. Then he heard faint muffled cries, mewing sounds. They came from a stand of aspen trees high up on the embankment. His ears flicked forward and he started toward the sounds. He crept slowly, a step at a time, as if he were stalking a bird. He sniffed the damp earth. A familiar smell filled his nostrils and he crawled closer. The thick underbrush and sun-dappled shadows limited his vision. But he knew the thing he was searching for was not far away. The muffled cries came again. Silently he pushed his way between the tangle of greenbriers. He lifted his head and peered into the shadows, his eyes adjusting to the dim light.

At first he saw only the leaf-littered interior, the mottled confusion of light and dark. Then, slowly, he made out the long, tawny shape, half hidden against the speckled floor. It was a lioness with three nursing cubs. Metan's body trembled. His small pink tongue flicked out and licked his dry lips. He moved forward silently, not daring to make a sound. The lioness was breathing lightly, her eyes closed as if she were sleeping. The cubs were intent on their feeding.

Metan crawled closer. He glanced around, his small black nose twitching. Quietly he wiggled his way in between two of the cubs. For a while he lay still, expecting at any moment to be cuffed and chased away. He waited, tense and watchful, ready to run. Slowly the lioness opened her eyes. She looked at him, then turned her head and sniffed him carefully from nose to rump, at the same time purring softly. Metan trembled and lay still. The lioness licked his face with her wet tongue. Then she yawned, laid her head down and went back to sleep.

Metan poked his nose into the warm fur and found

the free nipple. He prodded the dug with his paw and the warm creamy milk flowed into his mouth and filled his belly. Three times that day he nursed. By nightfall some of his strength was back and he had a warm sense of belonging.

As the weeks passed, Metan's blue-gray eyes turned to a deep amber. A few chestnut-colored rosette spots covered his face and shoulders, with one right in the center of his nose. He romped with the other cubs, wrestling and rolling in the prairie grass. He followed the lioness to the kills, where he grew fat on the soft belly meat of bison, and he learned to scrape the flesh from the rib bones with his rough tongue. He was still a cub, yet he followed the pride across the prairie and watched how they stalked and killed.

For over a thousand seasons this river pride had hunted and dominated the surrounding plains. The big males ruled for a few years, then were driven out by stronger, younger rivals. But the lionesses were the core of the pride, handing down the territory to their sisters, aunts and daughters. From generation to generation the pride was as enduring as the river and the cottonwood trees.

Within five months Metan was sleek and strong. Standing on long, sturdy legs, he resembled a half-grown cheetah. A thin, dun-colored mane began to grow over his tawny neck and shoulders. Like the other cubs, he had to share the kill of the adults and be satisfied with the leavings. Yet he soon learned to hunt on his own, tracking down marmots, ground squirrels, even lizards and bull snakes, anything that came within reach of his oversized paws.

Each morning in the gathering cool of twilight Metan set out to hunt. This morning he picked his way quietly along the river bottom, his amber eyes searching, his black nose twitching to pick up a scent. The big animals—the bison, the horses and the elk—were still much too large for him but he had outgrown his taste for marmots. Aimlessly he turned up through the buckthorns and peered over the embankment. A short distance away he spotted a small band of pronghorns out on the open prairie. Unaware of his presence, they grazed on the silvery leaves of leadplants and spiny cactus.

Metan hunched low, creeping forward slowly as the breeze blew up swirls of dust. He moved silently, blending in with the waves of yellow grass. He was lithe and fast but the antelopes were faster. He had to get within striking distance before they spooked and ran off, their white tail patches flashing in the morning sun.

He waited patiently, his body quivering tensely, his eyes fastened on the little band. The wind blew up a low howling moan, rustling the grass. Metan crept closer, stretching out one paw then the other, a tawny shadow flowing across the ground.

One of the pronghorns near the edge of the group acted as a sentinel, looking up every few moments to search the prairie, its black nose sniffing, testing the air. Off to one side a half-grown, orphaned fawn browsed alone. Head down, munching noisily, she was only half alert.

To that one Metan directed his attention. With his belly almost scraping the ground, he crept closer until he could hear the grazing beasts pulling the leaves of the leadplants out by the roots, until he could see the dung flies buzzing about their small hooves.

He gathered his legs beneath him and waited, the black tip of his tail switching nervously. Then, as the breeze came to him, he rose up and raced toward the unsuspecting antelopes. The sentinel caught the flash of tawny fur and barked, and the entire band whirled around and dashed off across the plains.

The fawn hesitated for a fraction of a second, then turned and raced after the fleeing band. Instead of dashing straight away, she panicked and ran at an angle. Metan gauged the distance well and within a dozen bounds their paths converged. Without missing a stride, Metan knocked her to the ground. She got up quickly but the young lion whirled around and caught her by the back of the neck and shook her hard, breaking her back.

For a moment Metan stood there, panting heavily, his pink tongue lolling out of his mouth. It was a small fawn, not much bigger than a jackrabbit, but it was his first important kill.

He glanced about, scanning the nearby hills to be sure other lions or dire wolves were not around, for he knew they would take the fawn away from him. He saw none and reached down and grabbed the dead antelope by the throat and dragged it into the tall grass. Hungrily he ripped open the gut and began to eat, gulping down long strips of tender meat.

He had not been feeding long when a huge shadow passed over him. He looked up to see Teratorn swooping down. The great bird landed nearby. He glanced around quickly and saw that Metan was alone. Then he waddled toward him with wings half open.

Metan got to his feet, snarling. He stood with one paw on the carcass, ready to defend it. Teratorn towered over him, glaring down with sullen threats, hissing and snapping his bill.

Metan stood firm. He spit back and bared his fangs in a warning snarl. But the huge bird waddled closer. Stretching out his long snakelike neck, he flew at Metan, striking viciously with his curved beak. With lightning-swift jabs of his sharp claws, Metan fought back, refusing to give up his prize.

Teratorn held up his wings to ward off the blows. Then he lunged forward, slapping Metan across the head and shoulders. The force of the attack drove Metan back, sending him rolling across the ground, dazed and confused.

Teratorn stood on the carcass, ready to carry it off. But Metan rushed in again. He leaped up, trying to grab the big condor by the neck. Once again Teratorn held up his wings, shielding his body. Then quickly he struck back, slashing the young lion across the face with his long, hooked bill.

Metan felt the stabbing pain as blood trickled down his forehead and into his eyes, blinding him. Teratorn waddled forward, batting the young lion with his wings, driving him still farther away from the carcass.

Metan lay in the grass, panting and blinking his eyes. Through a blur of vision he saw the vultures already gathering overhead. He heard the yap of a coyote, and he saw a big male lion standing on top of the rise. He knew they were coming.

Teratorn knew it, too. Quickly he picked up the small antelope in his bill and ran across the prairie on outstretched wings. He flapped for a moment, then caught an updraft and sailed into the sky.

Metan wiped his face with his paws and licked off the blood. He watched Teratorn soar away into the distance, the antelope fawn dangling from his bill. The young lion turned and loped off across the prairie. The next time he made a kill he would know enough to hide it under the trees.

7 · DROUGHT

ALL SPRING THE prairie grasses grew lush and thick and the herds prospered. Then in midsummer the afternoon skies turned azure blue, cloudless and hot. The scarlet mallow flowers carpeting the valley floor wilted along with the morning glories and butterfly weed. Slowly the face of the prairie changed.

The grass turned yellow, then brown, the brittle stalks rustling in the dry wind. Day after day the plants shriveled under the hot sun. The water holes and pan lakes dried up, and the animals began to congregate along the river bottoms. Hot, arid winds blew in from the west while swirls of dust devils sucked up the loose chaff and spun and danced it across the land.

The great herds of bison, horses and antelopes grazed endlessly back and forth across the land until the grass was chomped down to the roots. Now, with little forage left, they started out on a long migration in search of new pastures. They wandered south. In endless winding columns stretching far beyond the horizon they trekked over the low, rolling hills. Bawling and bellowing, the shaggy long-horned bison moved slowly, the bulls scattered singly or in small bachelor groups, the cows and calves bunched together on their own.

Bands of horses and elk trudged in and around them with clouds of yellow dust floating over their heads. On and on they wandered in a constant search for water and the life-giving grass. Flocks of cowbirds perched on the broad backs of the shaggy bison, while troops of great white storks strutted between the herds, snapping at insects, mice and lizards stirred up by the plodding beasts.

Even as the drought grew worse, the pounding hooves trampled the seeds of grasses and other plants into the dry earth, where they lay ready to germinate and bring forth new life with the coming of the first rains.

Hungry for fresh pastures, Kang drove his little band of mares and colts up near the head of the column. They were the first to miss the lush grass, the first to start the long trek.

Equus trotted along beside his mother, sometimes pressing against her to feel the closeness of her body. Each time they stopped to rest he nuzzled against her, seeking out her dugs to nurse greedily. But with the drought and lack of forage her milk was beginning to dry up and he was forced to nibble on plantain leaves

and shriveled tufts of bunchgrass to ease his hunger. Yet within four months he had grown strong and sturdy. He still galloped about, chasing the painted butterflies and the feathery, wind-blown thistle seeds.

Then, one afternoon, engrossed in his playful romps, he failed to see the ominous black clouds boiling up on the horizon. A strange chalky smell filled his nostrils and the air took on a hazy, yellow tinge. Gusts of wind howled out of the west and gradually thick black clouds rolled in, blotting out the sun.

Equus snorted and shook his head. He whinnied and galloped back to his mother. Frightened and uncertain, he pressed against her as a thick darkness slowly engulfed them.

Boiling clouds of dust rolled over everything, stinging the eyes, muffling the sounds of the clopping hooves and the bawling moans of the bison. A howling blizzard of dust and silt, it swept across the land, blanketing everything in its path.

Equus pinched his nostrils together to keep out the sand. He peered through slitted eyes but the grit was blinding and he saw only the darkness. The dust swirled around him. Instinctively he spread out his legs and turned his back to it.

The storm continued, filling his ears with its mournful wail. In the grim darkness he could sense the crowded shoving and pushing as the other horses and the bison milled around him. Then one of the beasts bumped into him, knocking him to the ground.

Quickly he got to his feet, bracing himself against the howling whirlwind. Particles of sand and silt pelted his face and shoulders. Black dust clogged his ears and caught in the corners of his eyes. He could see nothing. He could still hear the muffled stomping of hooves and the low moaning grunts of the bison. Yet they seemed fainter now, as if drifting farther away.

The thick dust continued to swirl around him as he shook himself and lowered his head, snorting, blowing through his nostrils. He moved from side to side to touch his mother, to lean against her, but he felt only the blast of the wind. Unable to stand against the pelting sand and grit, he folded his legs beneath him and lay on the ground, his neck stretched out in front of him.

For a long while he lay there trembling, waiting, pinching his nostrils tight against the chalky dust. He opened one eye to look around. The pelting sand stung his face and he quickly shut his eye again. As he lay there the darkness and the choking dust seemed to go on forever. He flicked his ears from side to side, listening. Then, slowly the howling wind seemed to die down and become a distant moan. He opened his eyes as the blackness faded to a dim yellow glow.

He pulled himself to his feet and snorted. Then he stomped his hooves and tossed his head to shake off the dust. He blinked his eyes and looked around. The land was ashen gray, desolate and deserted. The herds had disappeared into the distance. His mother was gone.

Panic gripped him. He was alone on the wide, empty plains. His legs began to tremble. Far off he could make out the lowering clouds of dust churned up by the migrating beasts as they moved along. He whinnied and shook himself again and galloped after them. He jumped over a big stork that lay trampled and broken on the ground, its white feathers covered with soot and dust. Nearby, a lost bison calf, half blinded by the storm, bawled and wandered about in circles.

Slowly the air cleared and the hot sun beat down with even greater intensity. Equus hurried along to catch up with the herds, certain that he would find his mother. He kicked up puffs of gray dust with every step. Now he could hear the bawling moans of the bison and soon he could make out their wide black horns swaying and bobbing in the sunlight.

Suddenly he saw a small band of horses trotting along near the edge of the herds. They were dun-colored like Kang and his mother. Fear left him and his spirits picked up. Quickly he galloped toward them, sure that his mother must be among them.

He had not gone far when two dire wolves ran out from behind a clump of cedar trees and blocked his way. His body stiffened and he stood there for a moment, frightened and uncertain.

He turned to run back but stopped as he saw three wolves loping up behind him. He glanced about and saw more wolves coming in from both sides. They were all about him now, a growling pack of hungry beasts.

In a fit of panic he galloped in a tight circle around the closing ring of wolves, looking for an opening. But wherever he turned a snarling beast stood in his way. He froze for a moment, waiting. Then, with a sudden lunge, he dashed ahead and leaped between two of the wolves in front of him. They jumped up at him but their snapping jaws missed and for a moment he broke free. Frantically he raced across the prairie, his hooves pounding through the dry grass. But the hungry wolves were right behind him, bounding over the dusty ground, ears laid back, tongues hanging out of their mouths.

Equus galloped hard, his eyes wide with panic. He saw two more wolves cutting across directly in front of him. He turned quickly to avoid them and once again found himself running in circles as one by one the wolves took up the chase, nipping at his legs, wearing him down.

He galloped around, dodging from one gray ghost to another as he looked for an opening. His hooves kicked up clouds of dust and he choked and wheezed from the dryness of it.

Panting and out of breath, he began to slow down. Then, once again he came to a stop, his chest heaving, his legs splayed out. He had run as far as he could.

The wolves, too, were winded. They pressed around him from all sides, heads low, tongues lolling out of the sides of their mouths. They were in no hurry now, their prey was surrounded.

With his head down, Equus stood there. His body was wet with sweat, his eyes wide with fear. Weaving back and forth, he struggled to keep his footing as the snarling, gray beasts crept toward him. Hurriedly he glanced around. Just beyond the ring of wolves he saw a large herd of bison, loping along slowly, crowded together.

For a brief moment Equus waited. Then with a frantic lunge he galloped toward the two wolves directly in front of him and leaped over their heads. They jumped up at him, springing for the throat. Equus landed on top of them. He struggled for a moment, then broke free and dashed straight for the herd of bison.

At the sight of the wolves the bison broke into a run. Equus galloped hard to catch up to them. He was almost there when he felt the stab of shearing pain as iron jaws clamped on his hind leg. He tried to pull away but he was held fast. Angry snarls and growls filled the air. Fiery jaws nipped him in a dozen places and he was smothered by the blur of grayish fur as the wolves swarmed over him.

In a fit of blind terror he squealed and thrashed. He broke free again, and without stopping he drove headlong into the stampeding herd of bison. There, with blood running down his leg, he galloped along with them, well hidden within the pressing mass of bodies.

Not daring to go in among the pounding hooves, the wolves were soon left far behind.

After a wild run the herds slowed down and settled

into a steady, plodding walk. Equus felt safe now. He limped along in the center of the herds, stopping now and then to rest a moment and catch his breath.

He stayed with them as the herds wandered south. Always hungry, he ate what little forage he could find. He learned to nibble on the dried tufts of grama grass and the shriveled leaves of the mallow and leadplants.

The wiry little pronghorns and camels fared better, thriving on the dried-up stalks of milkweed and the tough prickly pears.

Still searching for his mother, Equus approached each wandering band of horses. He sniffed at the brood mares and tried to nurse, but they squealed in anger, kicking out at him and chasing him away.

As the long days passed and he did not find her, he began to forget. Sadly he limped on. He became thin, his ribs showed through his dry skin and he staggered along under the hot sun, hungry and thirsty. He continued to nibble on the shriveled mallow leaves and the clumps of trampled clover, but these gave him little strength.

One morning as he stumbled along under the hot sun he became aware of a great shadow gliding along in front of him. Wherever he turned, it turned with him; whenever he stopped, it circled around him. That afternoon he looked up to see Teratorn soaring high overhead. The great condor was following him, waiting for him to die.

But Equus would not give up. Grimly he plodded on, staying near the middle of the herds, where there was less danger from dire wolves and prairie lions. Each day his head drooped a little more and he grew weaker. Sometimes he fell behind, then he trotted hurriedly to keep up with the rest of the herd.

During the day the hot sun beat down relentlessly, sapping his strength. But the nights were cooler and he lay down between the sleeping bison to rest and listen to the roaring of the prairie lions in the distance.

One morning the horses lifted their heads and began to whinny. The bison milled about restlessly, bawling and pawing the earth. Equus sniffed the air and smelled the dampness. Water was not far away.

Late that afternoon they came to the stream. It was almost dry but here and there were pools of murky water. The bison plunged in, crowding and shoving, eagerly sucking up the stagnant brown liquid.

Unable to push his way through the crushing mass of bodies, Equus wandered downstream and found a spot under the cool canopy of cottonwood trees, where the stream was covered with a mat of water lettuce. He waded in up to his belly. Pursing his muzzle, he pushed aside the floating water plants and drank long and deep. After hot days of trudging over dusty trails, the tepid waters felt cool and refreshing. He splashed through the water, shaking his head and shoulders, washing away days of grime and dirt.

The land was still gripped in drought but here, at least, there was some forage and water, and here the herds stayed to rest and regain their strength.

Equus ate water lettuce and browsed on the leaves of

sandbar willows. He stood up to his hips in the swampy backwaters, where the thick mats of algae helped to heal his bite wounds and the gash in his leg.

Five days later the herds began to move again. Revived by their short rest, they wandered south, in search of clear water and green grass.

Now that he could run and gallop, Equus joined a band of young stallions. Sensing fresh pastures ahead, they galloped across the plains. Equus kept up with them, his tail flying out behind him, his hooves thundering over the rolling brown hills.

8 ▴ THE SWARM

OLD MAMOOT GUIDED her little herd through the stubble of prairie grass. She had lived through many such droughts—hot, burning days that were etched in her memory as plainly as the floods, the prairie fires or the wintry blasts of ice and snow that penetrated her old bones and drove her south.

But she did not go south yet. Instead she took her family deep into the dry river bottoms. Here they pried off the bark of the cottonwood trees with their tusks and chewed on the green inner pulp for its nourishment and moisture. They reached up with long trunks and pulled down the low-hanging branches of the aspen and hackberry trees to feed on the tender twigs.

When they were thirsty the old matriarch guided them along the dried-up streambeds. In single file they lumbered beneath the canopy of willow trees. Walking in the lead, Ba swept the ground in front of her, sniffing back and forth over the sandbars and around the boulders with the tip of her trunk. Twice she stopped, testing the ground. Then she flapped her ears and moved on. Finally she paused over a wide expanse of bone-dry sand surrounded by large boulders. She rumbled in her throat and the old matriarch moved up beside her. They began kicking with their front feet, digging holes in the loose sand, scooping it out with their trunks. The other cows followed suit, each picking her own spot.

Huka stood beside the matriarch and watched as she continued digging, pushing the white sand away with her trunk. The hole deepened and slowly the sand began to change to a damp brown.

The little calf reached down and sniffed. He squealed with delight and ran about, swinging his trunk over his head while Mamoot continued to dig. Slowly a trickle of water welled up from the bottom. In his excitement, Huka came too close, toppling some of the loose sand back into the hole. The old matriarch pushed him aside gently, holding him back with her trunk as she dug some more with her foot. Then she stepped back and waited for the hole to fill with water.

But Huka, still impatient, leaned forward and poked the tip of his trunk into the brown puddle and blew up a froth of bubbles. Then he got down on his knees, curled his trunk over his forehead and tried to drink with his mouth. Once again a small avalanche of sand fell back into the hole.

Mamoot flapped her ears and grumbled softly. This time she pushed Huka well behind her while she patiently scooped out the wet sand. The hole filled with water again and the matriarch reached in and sucked up some of the brown liquid. She put the end of her trunk in the little calf's mouth and gave him a drink. Then she turned back to the pool and quenched her own thirst.

When they were finished drinking they splashed themselves with wet sand, tossing it over their heads and backs, feeling the cool goodness of it.

Day after day the sun beat down, scorching the prairie with hot, dry winds. Late one afternoon high black clouds piled up on the horizon. Slowly they drifted overhead, blotting out the sun. Moments later the rains came, huge pelting drops splashing onto the arid ground, each one kicking up puffs of dust. The dry earth sucked them up.

The mammoths lifted their trunks and waited for more. But no more came. Instead the black clouds passed on and disappeared toward the east. The sun came out and a steamy mist rose from the ground as the dampness evaporated into the hot air.

Two days later the air hummed with a curious vibrating sound. It throbbed and droned, first loud then faint, as if blown on gusts of wind. The matriarch shuffled uneasily. She turned toward the west and lifted her trunk as the strange whirring noise grew louder. The other cows turned with her, flapping their ears forward to catch the sound.

Like a thick brown cloud, it appeared in the sky. It

came closer and filled the air with a throbbing vibration, rolling and buzzing as it changed shape. First it was a tumbling mass of reddish-brown clouds, then it flattened out, stretching across the horizon in long, wispy strings. It swirled and boiled, coming together for a moment, then splitting apart again. The drone became a strident rasping sound, a throbbing buzz as if a million angry bees were flying overhead.

The mammoths looked up, confused and startled. Most of them had never seen anything like it before. But the old matriarch had seen it many summers ago, when the great brown cloud came out of the west and swept over the land.

And now it came again. It hovered above them, then settled down, a living curtain covering everything with its clattering racket.

But it was not one, it was many. It was an enormous plague of locusts, millions upon millions of grasshoppers, reddish-brown creatures each the size of a young willow leaf. Like a pelting hailstorm they landed all around the mammoths. They hopped about on stilted legs, rustling and fluttering their tissuelike wings.

Mamoot watched as the bustling insects rained all around her. They glinted in the sun like wet leaves falling after a rain. They hopped and crawled and struggled for room on the dry plant stems. They kicked and crowded each other. As they gnawed at the shriveled leaves, Mamoot could hear the grinding sounds of their tiny, serrated jaws.

More and more came. They rattled and hopped across the ground, clinging to everything in sight. By the hundreds they landed on Mamoot's head and back. They crawled up Huka's legs. The little calf trembled and squealed with fright. He ran to Mamoot, pressing against her. The old matriarch snorted and brushed them off with her trunk.

Endlessly the locusts came out of the west, settling down to feed. They clung to the cottonwood trees and hopped about in the willows and aspens. Their numbers weighted down the hackberries and elders, cracking the branches. They came in wave after wave, a living sea of ravaging insects, devouring every stalk of grass, every leaf in their path.

Harassed by the prickly creatures, the mammoths milled about in utter frustration. They stomped on the locusts, mashing them underfoot. They blew and slapped at them with their trunks. But it was no use; the annoying insects found their way into the mammoths' ears, into their mouths and eyes.

The huge beasts slapped and snorted, but they could stand it no longer. Trumpeting loudly, Mamoot led them up from the river bottom and out onto the open plains. Yet even here there was no escape from the pesky hordes.

For two days Mamoot kept the tormented beasts together as the grasshoppers stripped the trees bare and left the land barren.

Then, as quickly as they came, the locusts rose into

the air and flew off to the east. Now there was nothing left—no leaves, no grass, no tender twigs, and there would be nothing until the drought ended.

On the third morning Mamoot took her family back down to the river bottom. There they opened up the wells they had dug a few days before. She let them drink long and deep, and when they were ready she guided them south on a long trek, following the winding trails of the bison herds in a search for running water and fresh grazing land.

9 ▴ TAUG

YOUNG BULL TAUG had traveled far, plodding south through bone-dry country until he came to a new flat land where wide rivers flowed through lush grasslands and the air smelled like damp hay. Here the prairies rolled on in sweeping vistas of lush grass dotted with bright orange cornflowers and white primroses.

Teeming multitudes of grazing animals covered every hill and valley. Giant ground sloths browsed on the hillsides, their young ones close by, as they pulled down the heavily laden branches of yellow plum trees to get at the ripe fruit.

Taug moved on leisurely, his great bulk swaying as he strode through the knee-high grass. His trunk was in constant motion, sniffing the air, scratching behind his small hairy ear, tossing bunches of straw and dirt over his shoulders. At seventeen summers he was still young yet his leathery skin was cracked and gnarled like the bark of an old hackberry tree.

He still had fresh memories of his kin group, and he was lonely for the familiar smells, rumbles and touches of the once-friendly herd members. During his travels he encountered other family groups, young cows with calves and immature bulls led by an old cow or two. But he was not welcome among them and he was always driven off by the short-tempered old matriarchs.

One day Taug wandered into a group of four herd bulls; three of them were about his own age and not much larger than himself. But the fourth was Gundar the old patriarch, who was browsing noisily on the tender shoots of a coralberry tree nearby. His stomach growled and his temporal glands flowed profusely, the dark fluids running down the sides of his cheeks.

Taug noticed him but was not bold enough to approach a bull almost twice his size. Instead he advanced toward the three young herd bulls with his head high. In order to join them he would have to show submission or else tussle with them to prove his dominance, a behavior ritual that would determine where he fit into the group.

Blowing noisily, he swept his trunk through the tall grass and rumbled deep in his chest. He uprooted a small sumac tree and smashed it against the ground.

Gundar ignored the noisy youngster and continued with his feeding. But the other three bulls turned, eyeing the brash newcomer warily.

Taug lumbered up to the nearest bull. He lifted his head high and snorted a challenge. The other bull accepted, grumbling loudly, charging in with his head up. Their curved tusks met with a loud clatter, ivory clashing against ivory. They twined their trunks together tightly and shoved back and forth, testing each other's strength. Then they broke away and held up their heads, measuring their tusks in a bullish display of defiance. They circled slowly for a few moments. Taug moved in again but the other bull lowered his head, bowing and shuffling as he backed away in submission.

Before long a second bull came up to Taug and grumbled a challenge. This one was reddish-brown from wallowing in a clay bank. Snorting and blowing, they lifted their heads, still measuring their tusks. Once again Taug did not back down. Instead he quickly lowered his head and slammed into his opponent. Taken off guard, the red bull fell back. Taug rushed in again, this time wrapping his trunk over the other's forehead. He pushed hard, forcing the red bull back onto his haunches. When the red bull got to his feet Taug was waiting for him, ready to meet him head on. Then he was surprised as the red bull simply bowed and gave up the fight.

The third bull kept his distance, and Taug did not even bother to challenge him. He felt a new sense of power now. With little effort he had gained dominance over the group. Yet there was no closeness here, no rubbing of shoulders as there had been in his old matriarch family. Still he stayed with them, grazing and browsing beside them peacefully.

Then, late one afternoon, the herd came upon a

young plum tree. They gathered around it, pushing and jostling one another to get at the ripe fruit. Asserting his dominance rights, Taug shouldered his way in to a spot where the yellow fruit was easy to reach. He ate greedily, reaching high for the choice fruits and stuffing them into his mouth as the sweet juices dribbled down his chin. He had almost stripped the lower branches clean when a huge gray body bumped into him. In a quick fit of temper Taug spun around and slapped the offender across the face with his trunk.

It was Gundar the old patriarch, glowering down at him, his eyes blazing with fury. The old bull stepped back, then lifted his head high in an angry gesture. Taug stood there, unsure, startled by his own boldness. Only a few days before he had easily defeated the three young herd bulls. Yet this was a fight he did not seek, a challenge well beyond his strength and powers.

He started to back away but it was too late; the irascible old bull was determined on taking vengeance. He towered over Taug like a huge gray boulder. Then he lunged forward, his great curved tusks shining in the late-afternoon sun.

Taug braced himself, his head high, waiting for the impact. It came with a terrific crash. The enormous giant bowled into him, tusks smashing against tusks. He felt the shock vibrate through his legs and shoulders. An instant later their heads met with a solid crunch. Taug's ears rang with the clash. He saw flashes of light and he stood there swaying back and forth, stunned.

The old patriarch lifted himself high and made ready to charge again. Taug came out of his stupor just in time. He steadied himself and spread out his legs. At that moment the old bull crashed into him. There was a resounding crack and Taug felt a shearing stab of pain as his left tusk broke off and fell to the ground, leaving a section of raw nerve exposed.

Now the barrier of curved tusks that kept the great beasts from seriously hurting one other was gone. Left with a single tusk, Taug was a killer, a deadly weapon that would unwittingly penetrate Gundar's defenses.

In a rage of pain the young bull was more than willing to break off the fight and run away. But Gundar was already coming fast, pounding toward the young bull, his massive weight driving him on. He could not stop.

As Gundar came close, Taug lifted his head and braced himself and the old bull impaled himself on the single tusk. It entered high on his chest and plunged deep into his heart.

For a long moment the two bulls remained transfixed. Then the old patriarch stumbled backward, pulling himself off the young bull's red-stained tusk. He staggered in a circle, then crumbled to his knees, blood gurgling from the open wound in his chest. His eyes bulged and he rolled over on his side. He breathed once, twice, then closed his eyes and lay still.

Racked with a throbbing ache from the raw nerve of his broken tusk, Taug was completely unaware of his victory. Nor did he know that he had just killed his own father.

In a frenzy of pain he ran across the plains and down along the river bottom, slapping out at the willow saplings, tearing up water reeds and cattails, lashing out at anything that got in his way.

He waded in the warm marsh water, soaking his broken tusk. But it did little good; the throbbing pain persisted. Night came and he stomped about in a rage. He crashed through a thicket of sandbar willows, smashing them underfoot as he passed. He stormed up the embankment, where flecks of pale moonlight filtered through the leaves of the giant burr oaks. High above in the black canopy of branches a barred owl called, *Hoohoo hoowahoo.* It was answered by a mate far on the other side of the woods, *Hoowa whowahoo.*

Taug lumbered on, blowing and grumbling in pain, his stout legs shuffling across the leafy floor. Suddenly he heard a loud warning buzz. He looked around. Just in front of him, camouflaged by the dappled shadows on the forest floor, he saw the thick scaly body of a rattlesnake crossing his path. It was almost as fat as his trunk, and it turned quickly, facing him, its head held slightly above its coils, its black forked tongue flicking out in a tight circle. It held its head steady, the tiny pits below its eyes picking up the heat of Taug's body as its buzzing rattle continued to sound.

Crazed by pain, the young bull forgot caution. He reached out his trunk to sweep the huge reptile from his path. In that instant the snake struck. Two long hollow fangs sank deep into the fleshy tip of Taug's trunk and two venom-filled sacks injected a twin spurt of amber-colored fluid into the young bull's bloodstream.

The big snake recoiled quickly, its rattle still buzzing. Fuming with rage, Taug lifted his front foot and stomped heavily on the coiled snake, smashing it into the ground. For a few moments the reptile twisted and squirmed. Then its convulsions ceased, the sound of the rattle faded and it lay still.

All night long Taug stormed through the cottonwoods bordering the river, tearing up saplings, barging through the swamp reeds and cattails in an effort to rid himself of the terrible pain. The end of his trunk was swollen to twice its normal size, and he began to feel a strange dizziness. The potent venom raced through his veins, breaking down the red corpuscles, its effect speeded by his own wild exertions.

Morning light tinged the eastern sky as Taug came up out of the bottomlands and staggered across the prairie. His vision was blurred now, and he charged at the shadows of the young cedar trees as if they were the cause of his suffering. He barged wildly through the tall grass. Bison moved out of his way. Horses eyed him cautiously, and prairie lions slunk quietly into the greenbrier thickets.

But, not far away, two pairs of eyes watched him with interest. Two huge saber cats peered over the tops of the yellow grass, studying him closely. Long, deadly eight-inch fangs hung down from their upper jaws, sharp claws armed their massive paws. Normally a young bull mammoth was much too powerful for them to attack. But this bull was acting strangely.

The saber cats dropped down into the grass and slunk around to come up a short distance behind the young bull. There they waited patiently, gauging their chances for an easy kill.

By midmorning Taug staggered across the prairie to the shade of a huge old burr oak standing in the middle of the plains. His trunk was useless now, a swollen mass of throbbing pain. His eyes were bloodshot slits of light, and his legs were weak and unsteady. Breathing heavily, he leaned against the trunk of the massive old burr oak.

Now the saber cats came out of cover. The female approached warily, crouching low, creeping up openly to within a short distance of the injured mammoth. Then she reared up and growled.

Grumbling in pain and racked with fever, Taug seemed not to see her. He pressed against the oak tree, trembling in an agony of torment, unable to move.

It was time for the kill. The male saber cat sprang out of hiding. He dashed across in front of his mate and flung himself at Taug, his long fangs stabbing for the jugular in the young bull's throat. At the same time the female pounced on Taug's side, her fangs cutting deep between the ribs, opening a slashing gap into the chest cavity. It took but a moment, then the two cats jumped down and fled into the tall grass, where they watched and waited.

It did not take long. Bleeding profusely from his throat wound and unable to breathe, Taug slid to his knees along the trunk of the tree. He groaned feebly, then rolled over on his side and lay still.

The saber cats waited until they were sure the mammoth was dead. Then they trotted out into the open to claim their kill.

10 ▴ THE SCAVENGERS

THE BIG CATS sliced the carcass down the belly with their long, knifelike fangs. They devoured the liver and spleen, lapping up the blood. They ate huge chunks of soft meat from inside the thighs and groin. When they had their fill, they went off into the buckbush thickets to sleep, leaving the rest for the scavengers.

And the scavengers came; they came from far across the plains. They came on the currents of air and swooped down from the sky. They came up from the soil and out of the sod, from under stones and logs. They came on outstretched wings. They crawled and they crept in a hundred forms, for wherever there was death, they would find it.

The vultures were the first to arrive. They waddled around the carcass, tearing at the entrails and strips of belly meat. Giant storks picked out the eyes and stripped meat from the exposed ribs. Dire wolves came and chased them all away, then tore at the limbs and pulled out the tongue. They, in turn, were frightened off by a pride of prairie lions, who squatted shoulder to shoulder around the dead beast, feasting on the heart and lungs.

When the lions were through, the vultures and the dire wolves returned, accompanied by walking eagles, ravens and magpies. By midafternoon thousands of blowflies, dung beetles, roaches, flesh flies and yellow jackets flew in to feed or lay their eggs on the mangled carcass.

Darkness fell and the creatures of the night took over. Armadillos chewed and pulled on the strips of flesh still clinging to the almost-bare skeleton. Shrews and deer mice picked out bits of meat from the holes and crannies of the skull and backbone. Packs of wood rats gnawed at the cartilage and tendons between the bones. Spotted skunks arrived with a procession of young ones to join in the feast, while burrowing owls swooped down out of the darkness to catch the unwary shrews and roaches.

During the night carrion beetles dug their way out of the soil to come up under the carcass, chewing off bits and pieces, burying them under the ground to provide food for hatching larvae.

For three days and nights the banquet continued until the dead mammoth had all but disappeared, his body recycled back into the environment. A scattering of bones and a single tusk lay under the giant burr oak, all that was left to show that young bull Taug had ever existed.

11 ▴ THE STALLION

EQUUS HAD TRAVELED far south with the wandering herds of bison and camels. Here, within two years he grew tough and wiry. No longer a colt, strong muscles rippled under his smooth, nut-brown hide, and a short, bristling mane ran down the scruff of his neck. A restless urge stirred within him, and he left the band of young herd stallions to follow its call. He trotted across the grasslands, eyeing the roving bands of mares. Instinct told him it was time to round up a harem of his own.

Now, in the summer of his youth, he grew impatient. Early one morning as he drank by the river's edge, a band of four young mares ambled down to the opposite shore, all without foals.

Equus stopped and sniffed as a deep, musky scent drifted toward him from across the stream. It filled his nostrils with an enticing odor. He pawed the sandy bank restlessly as he watched them tossing their heads and swishing their shiny black tails.

The water was shallow and he stepped across lightly, neighing as he approached them.

The mares looked up, studying him. Their ears flicked forward, showing interest. Equus nickered. He stretched out his neck and stepped closer, almost within reach.

He got no farther. From a low rise of ground not far away a big dun-colored stallion galloped down the grassy slope, squealing wildly, his nostrils flaring. His big hooves pounded as he galloped. Heavily muscled, ear-torn and scarred from many battles, the old stallion rushed at Equus.

Equus jumped out of the way. But the dun horse turned quickly. With ears laid back he hurled himself at the young stallion, biting with stone-hard teeth. Equus stumbled back. He fell to the ground and rolled over, legs flying, hooves pawing the air.

Quickly he jumped to his feet, waiting. As the big stallion charged in again, Equus met him head on. He struck out with his sharp hooves. He nipped at the old stallion's ears and shoulders. He spun around and kicked savagely with his rear hooves.

But it did little good. The dun horse was strong. Time and again he charged in, biting Equus across the neck and face, throwing his heavy body against him, wearing him down.

Once more the dun horse rushed in, squealing wildly. With strong jaws he grabbed Equus by the back of the neck and shook him violently. Clouds of dust

rose up around them as their stomping hooves pounded the dry grass.

Equus struggled to keep his feet as the superior weight of the old stallion overpowered him. He fought back viciously, lashing out with his hooves. But each time the big stallion rushed in, Equus was thrown back. Cunning and battle-wise, the dun horse shoved and butted with his head, giving Equus no chance to get set.

They backed away and for a moment Equus stood there, panting heavily. Many times he had fought and sparred with other young colts, learning to dodge and kick, but it was mostly play. It had not prepared him for this.

Now Equus stood there, his legs spread out. Sweat covered his body, turning his coat black. He needed to rest, but the big stallion snorted and slammed into him again, knocking him off balance. Equus went down. His legs flew out from under him and he lay there breathing hard. Through the haze of dust he saw the big stallion rise up over him, ready to pommel him into the grass. Equus twisted hard and rolled out of the way just as the big stallion's front hooves hammered into the ground beside him.

Quickly Equus jumped to his feet as the dun horse rushed in again. But this time Equus did not wait. He spun around and galloped off across the prairie with the angry stallion nipping at his rump.

Equus galloped over the grasslands until he reached

the far end of the valley. There the dun horse gave up the chase. Equus stopped to catch his breath. He knew now he was not big enough to challenge the lead stallions and take over their harems.

Yet as the months passed he became impatient and instinct goaded him to try again. He ambled across the bluestem prairie, studying the mares from a distance as they grazed under the watchful eyes of their stallions. At times he was able to get close, peering from behind a stand of young cedars or watching from the crest of a nearby hill. But he always kept a sharp lookout for the lead stallions and galloped away if they grew suspicious.

Spring was almost over when one day Equus came upon a roan mare grazing off by herself. The lead stallion stood on a knoll a good distance away, surrounded by his harem of mares.

Equus felt his body tremble with excitement. He pranced and tossed his head as he took in the scene. It was a large harem. Many of the mares had foals, and Equus sensed it would not be easy for the stallion to keep them all in sight at the same time. He put his head down and began to graze in a wide arc, slowly making his way toward the roan mare. He glanced up occasionally to be sure the stallion was still at his lookout.

When he got close, the roan mare raised her head, startled. She turned slowly and started walking back toward the harem. Equus galloped in front of her, cutting her off. She dodged from one side to the other, but each time she turned Equus got in front of her and drove her back. Then she stopped, flustered and uncertain. Suddenly she turned and galloped toward the river. It was exactly what Equus wanted.

The lead stallion, fully alerted now, came galloping down, racing across the grasslands, hooves pounding, eyes blazing with anger.

Equus still had his attention on the mare, following her toward the river. Suddenly he heard the thundering hooves. He turned to see the big stallion right behind him. He heard the shrill squeal and felt the nip of flint-hard teeth on his rump. With a quick turn Equus let the mare go and veered off across the valley.

The lead stallion stopped. He stood there for a moment as if undecided. Then, instead of rounding up his mare, he turned and charged after Equus. They raced over the grasslands, pounding hard. Bands of grazing antelopes scattered out of their way. A group of gawking camels stood by and watched them pass.

Equus raced ahead without looking back, his hooves flying over the ground. Winded and blowing, the old stallion slowed down. He tossed his head and galloped back to his harem.

Equus stopped, his nostrils flaring as he shook himself, throwing flecks of white foam from his lips. He looked back over his shoulder, searching the far horizon. He did not see the roan mare.

The following morning he went down into the cottonwoods along the riverbank to drink. It was hot and a swarm of sulphur butterflies sucked at the thin crust of salt on the mud flats. Like a yellow cloud of leaves, they fluttered into the air as Equus splashed by. High overhead a flock of raucous crows mobbed a great horned owl sitting out the daylight in the shadows of an old cedar tree.

Then Equus smelled the familiar musky odor, and he heard the faint sound of a cracking twig. The wind was changeable and it was difficult to tell where the scent came from. He made his way up the bank and onto the prairie, dimly conscious of something following him.

Suddenly a reddish-brown figure walked out of the shadows and into the sunlight and stood in front of him. It was the roan mare. She whinnied softly and ambled toward him, stretching out her neck, sniffing. They touched noses and she rubbed against him. She was lithe and young and warm.

Equus nickered and brushed his muzzle along the side of her head, touching her ears and eyes. She lifted her head high and he nuzzled the underside of her neck. A moment later they walked side by side out across the prairie.

Unwittingly, Equus had found a way to round up a harem of his own. Whenever he came across a large band of horses with many mares without foals, he found that it was often possible to steal one of the mares while the lead stallion was watching the others. He tried it again and again. It did not work every time, but by the beginning of summer he had gathered a little harem of three mares and by the following spring he had two newborn colts.

12 ▴ THE LIONS

METAN, TOO, HAD grown strong and swift. As a nomad, he had followed the herds deep into this southland, a land of tall grass and wide rivers. Occasionally he pulled down a bison calf or a colt on his own, but mostly he scrounged the leftover kills of pumas, saber cats and dire wolves.

Like the dire wolves, Metan watched the skies. When he saw the big black scavengers glide to earth he hurried to the spot. Usually it meant food, sometimes great mounds of meat—dead bison, mammoths or mastodons. Though it might be smelly and slightly tainted, it made little difference.

As a social animal, Metan instinctively wanted a pride, a mate or a companion to help him hunt. So far he had found none.

This morning he loped across the prairie. He had not eaten in four days. The sun was just coming up and a bright tinge of light washed across the eastern sky. He had not gone far when he stopped and froze in place. A small band of horses grazed not far off, near the edge of the prairie. It was Equus and two of his mares, both with colts. A line of willow saplings grew off to the right between Metan and Equus. Metan crept behind them, sliding on his belly to get closer to the horses. There he began his stalk.

Equus trotted through the yellow grass in a small circle, nervous and watchful, yet unaware of the approaching danger. Two of his mares grazed peacefully in the open a short distance away, alongside their colts. But a third was lying down, half hidden in the shadows of a buckbush thicket, giving birth to a foal.

Metan's eyes were on Equus; he had not yet spotted the birthing mare. He moved up slowly through the willows and continued to stalk. When he crouched down, the bluestem grass in front of him was over his shoulders and he kept the top of his head just above it to keep the horses in sight. The wind was blowing toward him and he took advantage of it, moving up a step or two when it swayed the grass tops, hunching down when it stopped.

Soon he was close enough to see the scar marks on the young stallion's flank and legs. From the restless gait he sensed the young stallion was distracted. Something was wrong.

Equus continued his pacing, nickering softly, ever watchful. His eyesight was keen, his field of vision wide. With a slight turn of his head he could see behind

him as well as directly in front. But he did not yet see Metan crouched in the tall grass.

At the moment Equus was skittish. Not far away the birthing mare squirmed and moaned. Her delivery was stubborn and was taking longer than it should. The young stallion pranced around her nervously. Suddenly he stopped and lifted his head, sniffing the air as a strong feline scent filled his nostrils. He nickered softly as if telling the mare to hurry.

Little by little Metan crept closer, almost ready to spring. He held his head slightly above the grass tops to get a better view. The two mares were still off to the left, grazing with their colts. But Equus was directly in front of him, and he was the one Metan wanted.

Then Metan raised his eyes a bit higher and saw a tawny head, barely visible above the grass tops, just beyond the horses. It was another prairie lion, a male, and Metan was sure he, too, had his eyes on Equus.

Metan knew he could wait no longer. He was not as close as he should be but he would have to charge now if he wanted the kill. He pulled himself to his feet, his huge body in plain sight. With a wild lunge, he charged across the open space, a tawny shadow flying over the ground.

Equus saw him coming. He turned quickly. With a shrill squeal he alerted the rest of his band and galloped away, leaving the birthing mare where she lay. His colts and mares dashed off ahead of him, their hooves pounding hard over the prairie. Equus raced after them, driving them away from the approaching danger.

Metan tried to overtake them but the young stallion's band had a running start and widened the gap with each bounding stride. Heads bobbing, hooves pounding, they soon drew far ahead of the lion.

Metan stopped, his chest heaving, his tongue lolling out of his mouth. He knew he had made a mistake. He had been impatient; he had charged from too great a distance. Bristling with anger and still hungry, he loped back toward the buckbush thicket. Halfway there he saw the tawny lion. He was lying in the grass, his jaws clamped over the throat of the birthing mare, cutting off her wind. The stillborn foal, in its fetal sack, lay beside her.

Metan approached cautiously. It was not his kill but he was hungry. The two lions stared at each other for a long moment. Finally the mare breathed a final gasp and was dead. The tawny lion released his grip and walked around to the groin, where he began tearing and clawing at the soft underbelly.

Metan stepped closer. He was half starved and ready to fight for a portion of the kill if he had to.

The tawny lion slashed open the soft skin and began feeding on the viscera. Metan stepped closer. The tawny one snarled but continued feeding, his muzzle and long canine teeth stained with blood. Metan stood firm, his muscles tense, his lips curled back, ready to fight. Cautiously he put his paw out and laid it on the chest of the dead mare, watching the other lion for a sign of hostility. There was none. He waited another moment. Then he crouched down and began tearing at the soft flesh within the open belly.

While the lions were feeding, Equus came back. He stayed just out of reach, galloping about, whinnying and squealing in a nervous frenzy. But there was nothing he could do. It was too late to save his mare. Venting his anger with a final squeal of rage, he galloped off across the grasslands to join his little band.

The lions paid little attention to the frantic stallion. They were too busy grunting and slobbering, eating greedily side by side. They ate until their bellies were heavy with meat, then they pulled the carcass deeper into the thicket, where they could guard it from scavengers, leaving the stillborn colt for the hungry vultures already circling overhead. They licked their bloody jowls with long pink tongues and stretched out in the grass. Metan closed his eyes and slept. His new hunting companion lay in the shade close beside him.

13 ▴ THE RETURN

SEASON AFTER SEASON the great herds grazed and browsed over this vast southern prairie land. In their teeming millions they spread out over the hills and valleys for a hundred miles or more. The long-horned bison, together with myriad bands of horses, cropped the bluestem grasses down to a stubble. Camels and antelopes thrived on the stubble, then ate the thistles and cacti, too.

Now, after three years of chomping teeth and pounding hooves, the land was played out, trampled into tufts of dried grass and straw, and once again the herds wandered in search of new pasture.

To go south would soon bring them to the sea. To the east were the forests, to the west the high mountains. But these bison, horses and camels were creatures of the prairies and open plains. Grass was their life, so they turned north, on a long, winding journey to find it.

This migration wasn't new, and it wasn't seasonal. In the north it happened sporadically, triggered by fire, flood, drought, plague or overgrazing. Then the great herds turned south, only to return north again in a few years. It was a natural cycle that had been going on for thousands of years.

Even now, as the herds started their long journey back, the drought in the north had ended. The heavy rains had come and the seeds that had been trampled into the earth three years before had germinated, covering the land with clover, goldenrod and billowing waves of prairie grass.

For Equus the journey began when he noticed scattered bands of horses turning away from the dry grasslands and slowly ambling out along the old trails leading north. He lifted his head and smelled a faint hint of dampness drifting toward him on the north wind. He tossed his head and whinnied. Then he rounded up his little band of mares and colts and drove them in its direction.

Soon all of the herds, the bison and camels, the antelopes and elk, were on the march. Bawling and bellowing, they plodded north, eight or ten miles a day, following the dusty trails their ancestors had etched into the earth over aeons.

To Metan and his tawny hunting companion the grass was only a place to hide, a place to lie in wait. The herds were the meat of life, so wherever they went Metan and his companion followed. Now, as the mi-

gration got under way, they prowled along the out-
skirts of the grunting, milling throngs. They pulled
down the weak and injured stragglers and ate the many
foot-weary beasts that fell along the way.

To Teratorn, as to Metan, the herds meant food. On
great outstretched wings ten feet across, he could soar
a hundred miles a day, following wherever they went.

Mamoot and her family of mammoths were among
the last to leave. They thrived for a few days in the
bottomlands, along the streams, browsing on the bark
of the cottonwood trees, on river grapes and willow
shoots. But soon even they were caught up in the mass
exodus.

Mamoot and Ba and some of the other cows had
made the trek many times before. Now they lifted their
trunks high over their heads, sniffing the air, and
climbed up onto the open prairie. They followed the
bison trails, walking in single file with great sweeping
strides that carried them over the ground swiftly. Huka
was four years old, growing slowly, still little more than
a calf. Like the other calves, he often had to run to keep
up. Within two days they caught up with the slow
plodding bison.

Now, far in front of her, Mamoot could see the great
masses of migrating beasts stretching to the horizon.
Like meandering columns of brown ants, they toiled
over the gently rolling hills. They waded across the
winding streams and through the stands of young
cedar trees scattered in the valleys.

Ba had her two-year-old calf now and she kept it safely beside her as she led the way, constantly caressing it, touching it with her trunk. Sometimes they caught up to bands of horses that had stopped to graze on clumps of dry grass and sedges or whatever forage they could find. In a patient, steady stride, Ba passed them by, her head bobbing gently from side to side as she listened to the rumbling commands of the old matriarch walking near the center of the column.

They stopped during the heat of the day to browse on the shoots of plum trees and to rest in the shade of drooping elms. In the cool of early evening they started out again, jogging another seven or eight miles before stopping for the night.

They stopped in the middle of the prairie and gathered in a tight circle with the calves in the center. Here they slept and rested. Huka closed his eyes and listened to the soft moans of the bison that lay in the grass nearby, chewing their cud. He heard the mournful howl of dire wolves as they lurked along the edge of the herds. He wrapped his trunk around the old matriarch's front leg and pressed closer.

Early the next morning Mamoot lifted her trunk and tested the wind. The smell of dampness was stronger now, a promise of lush pastures not too far away. She rumbled deeply in her throat, and the little family started out again in single file.

All morning they traveled, their pillarlike legs tramping over the dry, crumbling grass. Then far ahead, just within sight, stood an old burr oak, its twelve-inch leaves fluttering in the wind, its branches reaching eighty feet high. It was the great oak under which Taug had died two years before, and now a scant number of his bleached bones lay scattered in the dust beneath it.

Ba hurried along, her head swinging, her trunk reaching out, sniffing the ground ahead of her. In slow, easy strides she lumbered under the great oak. She had almost passed it when suddenly she stopped. She saw the bones and touched one with the tip of her trunk, fondling it. The other cows crowded around her. They poked at the crumbling ribs and broken sections of backbone. They snorted and flapped their ears.

Mamoot came up, grunting and blowing. She pushed her way into the middle of the herd and sniffed at the bones. Then she walked around them, rumbling in her throat, coiling and uncoiling her trunk. The other cows picked up pieces of the skeleton and carried them about, snorting and blowing.

But Mamoot knew more. Something about the lingering odor aroused her memory. She touched each bone, one at a time, with the tip of her trunk. She picked up a rib and held it high as she swayed back and forth, at the same time rumbling deep in her throat.

Ba coiled her trunk around a large section of crumbling backbone. She held it up as if showing it to the others. They reached out and touched it, feeling the dry, chalky texture. An ancient impulse overcame them. They walked around the bones, pushing gently, crowding together. They uncoiled their trunks and scooped the bones into a pile. They tore branches and leaves from a nearby elder shrub and scattered them over the bones.

When that was done, Mamoot began poking around the old burr oak, blowing and sniffing with her trunk. She thrashed about as if in anger, stomping through the tall grass that grew around the tree. Ba and the rest of the herd looked on, waiting. Suddenly the old matriarch let out an earsplitting trumpet. A moment later she came out holding a long, curved tusk in her trunk. The entire family rushed up to her. They gathered around, touching the tusk, squealing and rumbling. The tusk was yellowed and badly weathered, the ivory etched and scarred where it had been chewed by wood rats and porcupines.

Mamoot lifted it high over her head, then gently laid it across her own tusks, holding it in place with her trunk. She rumbled a command and Ba started out again with the little family strung out behind her. Mamoot marched in the middle of the column, her huge legs lumbering across the prairie, with the long, curved tusk in her trunk.

They traveled fast, covering thirty miles a day. The smell of water was strong now and fresh green grass began to appear all around them. Many of the bison herds had already stopped and spread out over the land to graze and to rest.

Two days later Mamoot and her family reached

home and now, all around them, a sea of waving grass covered the hills and valleys.

Great flocks of mallards and green winged teal flew in from the south and settled on the newly filled pan lakes while gray, red-capped cranes danced and rattled a loud cacophony of greeting. Everywhere the land and the waters teemed with new life.

Mamoot had not eaten since she found the big tusk. She would not put it down. But she let her family stop to graze on the lush fields of new clover. Next she took them down to a little glade of sandbar willows near the bend in the river. She began scraping away the sand with her front foot. The other cows saw what she was doing and began to help. They scooped and scraped until they had dug a long, shallow trench. When it was ready Mamoot leaned down and gently placed the broken tusk in the bottom. Huka and the calves looked on while Ba and the other cows scooped sand into the hole until the tusk was completely covered. For a moment they hovered over the spot. Then Mamoot rumbled deep in her throat and the little herd turned and went up onto the open prairie. They made their way between the bison and horses and stopped in the middle of the prairie. Here they began grazing, pulling up bunches of the new spring grass and stuffing them into their mouths. Huka leaned against the old matriarch as he ate, the sweet green juices dripping down his chin.

14 ▴ SPRING

ALL ACROSS THE PLAINS the bison bulls roared and fought, clashing horns for dominance over the young cows. They tore up sod and crashed through thickets of greenbriers, trampling them into the ground. In the scattered clumps of red cedar, pronghorn fawns were being born, and in the stands of tall grass, killdeer and meadowlarks were building their nests. Another spring had come to the prairie.

Like nomads, Metan and the tawny one had followed the herds north. By nature they were social animals and now, fully grown, instinct told them what to look for. Day and night they prowled the grasslands, searching constantly. They smelled the acrid urine markings sprayed over the yucca plants and heard the deep-throated coughing roars of the other prairie lions, all of which meant: This territory is taken.

Spurred by these warnings, they traveled on, from one area to another, stealing kills when they could, hunting when they had to, always searching for a place to settle down.

Then, early one morning, they found what they were looking for. They first saw the old male lion lying in the sun as they prowled around the edges of his territory. They watched patiently and soon the three mature lionesses in his pride loped into view. There were no cubs.

For seven days Metan and his companion loitered nearby, watching for other males. They saw none and they knew the old male ruled alone. Each night they heard him roar. It was weak and broken, ending in short, guttural grunts.

The next day, with the sun already high in the heavens, Metan trotted into the territory. The old one saw him coming. He pulled himself to his feet and groaned wearily. With ragged mane and ears tattered from many battles, he stood there glowering at Metan, waiting for him. Clouds of blowflies buzzed around him, attracted by the bleeding sores on his head and neck.

Metan stepped closer. He snarled, his black lips curled up over his sharp fangs. The old lion growled back, eyes glinting savagely, ready to fight. They circled slowly, glaring at each other. Metan's claws moved in and out of their sheaths nervously. He stepped closer until he and the old lion were barely inches apart, spitting, snarling in each other's face. The hair on the ridges of their backs bristled in anger.

Suddenly Metan reared up, lashing out with lightning-like blows of his big paws. The old lion struck back, growling, venting his fury. But he was slow. Metan sprang aside, dodging out of the way. They circled again, turning slowly, padding down the damp grass, each waiting for the other to strike again.

Metan made the move. He rushed in, flinging himself at the old lion. They clawed at each other, tumbling over the ground, growling in violent rage. In a blur of yellow haze, tufts of fur and grass flew up around them. Metan tried for the throat but the old lion shook him off. They broke free and backed away.

For a moment it was quiet as they sat facing each other, panting heavily. Then suddenly Metan's companion crashed out of the tall grass and threw himself on the old lion's back, sinking his teeth into the neck muscles and tearing out clawfuls of drab brown fur. At the same time Metan rushed in, raking the old one's shoulder with sharp claws, biting him in the face and neck, opening a deep wound on the cat's cheek.

The old lion whirled around, trying to throw off the attackers. But they swarmed over him, keeping him off his feet, clawing and ripping deep gashes in his back and shoulders.

The old one kicked and squirmed and managed to shake them off, and for a moment the three cats sat in the blood-stained grass glaring at each other. Now more blowflies gathered, buzzing around their heads, attracted by the oozing blood. Two vultures landed nearby, their naked heads bobbing up and down, waiting for the kill. The old lion was a pitiful sight now, his pink tongue hanging out as he panted, his bloodshot eyes narrow red slits in his shaggy old head.

Just then two of the lionesses came out snarling, as if ready to fight. Metan lunged at them, jabbing at one then the other with savage swipes. They backed away slowly. Then with heads lowered they retreated into the shadows of the nearby cottonwood trees.

Quickly Metan turned his attention back to the old cat, now crouched in the grass facing the tawny one. Without waiting, he charged from behind, clamping his jaws on the back of the old lion's neck, his sharp fangs sinking deep into the backbone.

Instantly Metan's companion jumped in, raking the old one's face and shoulders, his claws coming away with tufts of fur, his teeth red with blood. The three animals rolled over and over, crushing the high grass as their angry snarls filled the air.

Then, overpowered and badly beaten by the relentless attack, the old lion lay still. Suddenly all was quiet. Metan and his companion got to their feet and backed away as the old one lay stretched out in the grass, his ribs heaving. He groaned in pain and lifted his head. Metan and the tawny one paced around him.

With a great effort the old cat sat up. Trickles of blood dripped down his face. He blinked his eyes in the bright sun and looked around as if Metan and his companion were not even there. Slowly he pulled his back legs up under him and struggled to his feet, weaving back and forth.

Once more Metan started forward. Then he stopped. The old lion held his head low. With a last weak growl of bravado he limped off across the prairie.

The three lionesses stood under the shadow of the trees and watched him go. Metan followed the old lion, escorting him out of the territory to be sure he did not turn back.

That night far out on the grasslands the old one lay down under a lone cedar tree. He rested awhile, then tried to get up, but he could not. The wounds in his backbone had stiffened and paralyzed his legs. With one eye swollen shut, he could barely see. All he could do was lie there, nursing his pain, listening to the cries of the coyotes and the woeful *coo-cooing* of the burrowing owls.

That is the way the dire wolves found him, just before dawn. Half conscious, all but dead, he did not fight back. With powerful jaws they tore him apart. They ate what they could, then went home to their dens in the buckbush thickets, where they regurgitated part of their meals to feed their cubs.

When the sun was high, Teratorn came, together with the vultures and storks. What they did not eat they left for the coyotes and the carrion beetles.

That night Metan and his companion lifted their heads to the stars and roared loud and strong. The thundering sound carried far into the night. And from out of the darkness came an answer from another pride far across the river.

Metan lay stretched out under the purple sky, licking

his wounds. He and the tawny one had found their territory and won their pride. Now they would have to defend it, as the other lion had done until he became too old.

While Metan and his companion lay half asleep in the tall grass, the three lionesses walked out of the shadows and stood beside them. They snarled softly, a sign of acceptance. Then they loped off across the prairie. Tonight the females would hunt. If they were lucky enough to bring down an old bison cow, a horse or even a camel, Metan and the rest of the pride would eat well tomorrow.

15 ▴ OLD AGE

MAMOOT PLODDED SLOWLY through the lush grass, four attendant cowbirds climbing over her back and shoulders. All around her the prairie was in bloom. Mounds of white clover grew in the valleys. Lush meadows of bluestem grasses covered the hillsides. Red-tailed bumblebees buzzed around the globe mallows and morning glories, attracted by the red-and-blue blossoms and the sweet scent drifting on the warm morning air.

It was a time for good forage, a time for contentment. But Mamoot did not feel it. Instead she felt old and tired, the strain of six decades aching in her bones. Thirty years ago she had become the matriarch of her family, guiding it over the rolling plains and through the winding river forests. One year alone she had watched over as many as twenty-four cows with their young ones without losing a single calf to the saber cats or prairie lions. But that was long ago.

It was three years now since Mamoot and her herd

of mammoths had returned to this homeland, three years without plagues, droughts or dust storms.

This morning the old matriarch stood in the middle of the prairie while her little family grazed peacefully around her, cramming quads of grass into their mouths, their long, curved tusks shining white in the sunlight. Huka still grazed close beside her. He was seven years old now and seven feet high. Although he was long since weaned and could easily feed himself, by mammoth standards he was barely out of calfhood.

The old matriarch coiled her trunk around a thick tuft of long grass and tore it out of the ground. She slapped it against her front leg to knock off the dirt, then put it into her mouth. She chewed slowly, rocking back and forth. Abruptly she spit out the pulp, shaking her head in grumbling frustration. She pulled up another tuft of grass and started to put it into her mouth. Then she dropped it. It was fresh and green, but something was wrong. Even though she chose the tenderest shoots, the more she ate the more her stomach twisted in pain. Every day it grew worse, a gnawing, burning feeling deep in her gut. The only way she could ease the ache was to stop eating. So she stood there listlessly, half asleep, while Ba and the others went on with their feeding.

She had no way of knowing it, but after sixty years of chewing on tough grasses, leathery leaves, twigs and bark, her last set of molars were worn down to nubbins. They could no longer grind up the food, and her old gut could not tolerate the raw grass and foliage.

Huka sensed the change in the old matriarch and he pressed close to her. He reached up with his trunk and pushed a clump of fresh clove into her mouth, as if to help her. She shook her head and let it fall to the ground. Huka continued grazing, chewing on the clover and lush grasses as the sweet, green froth dripped down his chin.

For five days Mamoot moped about while the others fed. Finally she lumbered over to where Ba was feeding. She leaned against her and lifted her trunk, touching Ba around the ear, at the same time rumbling softly. Ba rumbled back and laid her own trunk across the old one's neck. They stood this way for a moment. Then, with her head drooping, Mamoot turned and walked slowly toward the river, leaving Ba to take care of the little family.

Huka squealed and ran after her. Mamoot snorted angrily, telling him to stay with the herd. But the young bull continued to follow. Mamoot butted him with her head and tusks, pushing him back. Still Huka refused to obey. Finally, too tired to resist any longer, the old matriarch let him accompany her.

They went down through the cottonwood trees and followed the riverbank until they came to the swamps. Here the stream flowed quietly, winding its way through the marshlands. And here Mamoot found what she was looking for: lush green mats of water plantain and pondweed. Hungrily she reached out with her trunk and swept up clumps of the tender green leaves. They were soft and spongy and easy to chew, and she filled her stomach with the tender plants. She felt better now, and within a few days she regained much of her strength.

Because of her great weight, Mamoot was careful to stay away from the soggy areas, where she might sink in and become bogged down in the mud. But Huka was lighter. Less fearful, he splashed recklessly through the shallows, pulling up cattails and water lilies and chasing herons. Yet he never went far beyond sight of the old matriarch.

Here, with the abundance of tender forage, the old matriarch could survive. Side by side, she and Huka spent their days basking in the warmth of the early-morning sun or cooling off under the shadows of the sandbar willows. Here, they listened to the ospreys scream as the big fish hawks built their nests high atop the dead cedar trees. They heard the guttural rattle of the marsh wrens and the *oooh chereeee* calls of the red-winged blackbirds as they bobbed and swayed on the long cattail stems.

Meanwhile, out on the open prairie Ba led the little family herd back and forth across the grasslands, guiding them as Mamoot had taught her to do. She took them to their old familiar haunts, to the pan lakes to bathe and drink, to the cottonwood forests to rest and cool off. Every few days Ba guided them into the swamps to visit Mamoot. There the big cows pressed around the old matriarch, putting the tips of their trunks in her mouth, caressing her, gently clanking their tusks against hers. Huka ran about, filled with excitement, greeting the yearling calves and entwining trunks with the older ones. Sometimes they stayed all day, sometimes only for a few hours.

Each time they left, Mamoot urged Huka to go with them. She scolded him with deep-throated grumbles and butted him with her head. But Huka balked and refused to leave his old friend. He stayed behind, squealing and snorting as he watched the mammoths lumber out of the swamps and disappear into the distance.

It wasn't long before the little family became accustomed to Ba as their new matriarch. They obeyed her willingly and came to depend on her as she walked near the center of the column with a big cow in the lead. She took them to the best feeding grounds, where the grasses were fresh and green. She guided them through the long valleys and to the chokecherry glades, where the bushes and plum trees were heavy with fruit.

During the midday heat they ambled down to the river. There the cows bathed and wallowed in the mud while the young calves splashed one another with water or chased the antelopes as they came down to drink.

It was a tranquil life, a daily round of grazing, sleeping and play. Because of their huge size they were rarely threatened. Except for an occasional attempt by a saber cat or a prairie lion to pull down a straying calf, there was little to disrupt their peaceful existence.

Then, one morning, a new predator appeared on the prairie. There were many of them and they came down from the north—tall, birdlike creatures that walked on two legs, like storks or herons. Without fangs, without claws and almost naked, they seemed vulnerable and harmless.

Ba noticed them when they were a long way off. Her trunk went up high over her head and she caught their scent on the early-morning breeze. It was an unfamiliar odor, one that she had never smelled before, and there was something about it she did not like. She flapped her ears and snorted as they came closer. They carried long, sharp-pointed sticks and like a band of bronze beasts they strode in the sunlight, pushing their way through the waist-high grass.

Ba rumbled quietly, her eyes on the approaching strangers. The cows and calves gathered around her. They lifted their trunks and sniffed the air. Now they, too, caught the peculiar odor. It did not smell like a saber cat or a prairie lion. It was different, a strong, pungent odor that lingered deep in the nostrils.

Boldly Ungog came down the hill, wading through the high grass. He stopped and pointed as the rest of his band caught up to him. He had seen mammoths many times before, great woolly beasts from up north. But these were much bigger and without hair.

Their tusks were longer and curved inward. Yet they were still mammoths, clumsy, stupid beasts, easy to kill. If they could wound one of the cows and follow it until it fell, they would have enough meat for many days.

Ungog raised his arm and started forward. The hunters followed, some holding spears, long, pointed sticks, ready to throw. Others carried large jagged stones in their hands.

Ba waited as the strange creatures came directly toward her family. The cows grew restless and Ba kept them close together. The calves huddled in the middle of the herd, peering out between the cows to watch the strange beasts. Suddenly one of the calves, overcome by curiosity, dashed out, flapping his ears and squealing, ready to chase the curious birdlike creatures. But the strange beasts did not run away as the storks and herons did. Disappointed, the little calf stood there, baffled.

Ungog grinned and stepped closer. This was going to be easy. Even the woolly ones up north knew enough to keep their calves behind them. He picked out his best spear and lifted it high over his head. He moved slightly to one side, aiming for the heart, just behind the shoulder. Then, with a mighty heave he threw his spear.

At that moment the calf turned and the spear struck him a glancing blow high on the shoulder. In shocked surprise, he squealed in fright and raced back to Ba and the family, a trickle of blood running down his shoulder.

Ungog grunted in disgust and picked up his spear. He looked at the mammoths as his companions gathered around him. The herd is small, he thought, we can still get a calf or one of the old cows. He looked around the ring of bronze faces staring at him, waiting for him to say the word. He studied the herd again. Then he raised his spear. "Go," he grunted. Shouting and yelling, the hunters turned and ran toward the mammoths.

Ba stood facing them, her little family close behind her. Anger surged in her breast. These creatures were not large. She could trample them into the dust as she would a lion or a dire wolf. She rushed forward, stomping her feet, raising a cloud of dust and trumpeting loudly to frighten them off.

Ungog and his companions stopped. They waited, but when they saw the big mammoth hesitate, they started forward again. As they came within range they began to throw their spears.

This time Ba did not stop to threaten; she charged straight at them, her eyes burning with hate.

Ungog threw his spear. It struck Ba on the forehead and fell to the ground. It opened a small cut and blood trickled down into her eye. She stopped and shook her head.

It gave Ungog and his hunters time to run.

Quickly she recovered and came on again. In a blind

fury, she charged after the fleeing beasts. But they had scattered in all directions. Confused and baffled, she stopped again, not knowing which one to chase. She stood there shaking herself, stomping and snorting.

Still trembling with anger, she ran back to the herd and took them far across the prairie, away from the strange beasts. With heads bobbing, the little family ran bunched up, crowded together, feeling a sense of security in their closeness, the hateful odor still lingering in their nostrils. They ran until they came to the river. There they waited in the shadows of the cottonwood forest until they felt the danger had passed.

16 ▲ AMBUSH

UNGOG AND HIS band roamed across the prairie hunting antelopes, camels and bison. They picked plums and hackberries along the riverbanks and caught snow geesc around the shores of the pan lakes.

But this morning Ungog hunted alone. He carried a long, sharp stick as he walked along the edge of the swamp. With head down, he scanned the sandbars, searching for a broad wavy track leading to the shallow water. When he found one he studied the place where the track began. There the sand was loose, as if it had been recently dug up. Ungog jammed his stick into the spot, probing. Each time he pulled up the stick he felt the tip with the end of his fingers. The third time he pulled it up the point was covered with a thick, viscous fluid.

Ungog smiled. He dropped his stick, then knelt down on his knees and began digging with his hands. A moment later he found what he was looking for—a clutch of white, leathery eggs, the nest of a snapping turtle. Ungog scooped them out, one by one, piling them alongside the hole.

He was almost finished when he heard grunting and the sound of splashing water not far away. Quickly he picked up his stick and left the eggs where they were. He waded into the swamp, up to his knees in water, hoping to spear a deer or perhaps a pig stranded in the bog. The wind was blowing toward him, and now along with the sloshing water he heard more grunts and rumblings. Carefully he parted the reeds and peered through. There, within the curtain of mist rising from the water he saw Mamoot and Huka feeding in the cattails. He stood for a while, watching and listening. He heard no other sounds and he knew the old cow and the calf were alone.

The sun was high when Mamoot first noticed the strange, pungent odor. She lifted her trunk over her head and sniffed the air. She had smelled it faintly early that morning but now it seemed to be all around her.

Huka smelled it, too. He sensed the old matriarch's concern and he stayed close to her.

Then they heard the sounds of footsteps splashing through the shallow water, coming in their direction. Loud shouts and cries filled the air as the steps came closer. Mamoot lifted her trunk again. The strange odor was stronger than ever.

Mamoot shook her head and snorted. The cowbirds on her back darted into the air and flew away.

The old matriarch nudged Huka. Together they turned and stomped through the cattails, moving deeper into the swamps to get away from the annoying sounds and smells. Then they waited, ears flapped forward, listening.

For a while all was quiet. But soon the shouts and the splashing sounds came again, and Mamoot knew they were being followed. Even here they were not safe. Confused and frustrated, she raised her trunk and trumpeted a loud warning. Then she and Huka plunged ahead, making for the open prairie two hundred yards away, where they could run and escape these pesky strangers.

But they had gone only a few steps when they heard the beasts directly in front of them. In a fit of rage Mamoot slapped the water with her trunk. She whirled around in the opposite direction and went crashing through the cattails, taking Huka far back into the swamps. She reached a marshy area overgrown with high reeds and patches of bog moss. There she stopped and braced herself and waited for the offensive, two-legged creatures.

They came a moment later, twenty-five or thirty of them, splashing through the swamps, up to their knees in water, their brown bodies glistening wet in the sun. Shouting and calling to each other, they stalked around the clumps of grass like a troop of giant birds searching for prey.

Ungog led the band. He waded ahead cautiously,

staring up at the massive beast. Step by step he waded closer, holding his spear high over his head, ready to throw.

The old matriarch bellowed with rage. She lifted her trunk and shattered the air with an ear-splitting trumpet. Then she tried to charge. But her great body refused to move. In her frantic rush to escape, she had blundered into a mass of floating bog moss. Now her back legs were mired deep in a spongy marsh. Desperately she tried to pull free, but her struggles served only to sink her deeper into the morass.

Ungog watched the great beast closely as he waded nearer. Any minute he expected her to attack. He waited. Then, suddenly he realized she was trapped, unable to charge. Boldly he stepped closer and drew back his arm. With a loud grunt he hurled his spear. It flew through the air and struck Mamoot in the chest, its sharp point driving deep into her flesh.

The old matriarch bellowed in pain. She reached down with her trunk and pulled out the spear and flung it to the ground.

Huka stayed a few feet behind Mamoot, shaking with fear. His small tusks were strong and sharp, and he towered over these strange beasts. Yet he was terrified by them. He wanted to get close to Mamoot, to hide behind her, but he was afraid to step into the patch of floating bog moss.

Mamoot thrashed about, lashing out with her trunk to get at her enemy, but she could not reach them.

She held her head high, her great sweep of curving tusks glinting yellow in the sunlight, her tiny eyes burning with hate. Again she lifted her trunk high over her head and let out an ear-splitting trumpet that blasted across the damp swampland. A behemoth, full of rage and fury, she stood there helpless before her puny tormentors.

Now Ungog stepped aside as the other hunters came up to throw their long sticks. Even though Mamoot was shackled by the thick mud, the hunters were intimidated by her great size. They stepped up hesitatingly and threw their spears, then quickly ran back out of reach. Most of the sticks missed and fell into the swamp reeds. One struck Mamoot on the shoulder, another grazed her front leg. Maddened by the pain, the old matriarch trumpeted in anger as she floundered in the soft bog.

More hunters came up with jagged stones. They ran up around the old matriarch, pommeling her from all sides.

Huka cringed in the background as the sticks and stones flew through the air. He crashed through the swamp reeds, squealing and trumpeting, lashing about with his trunk. Suddenly one of the sticks came from behind and struck him a glancing blow on the rump. For a long moment the young bull stood there trembling. Then slowly the stabbing pain shook him out of his fear and his terror turned to rage. Out of the corner of his eye he saw his attacker. He spun around just as the hunter was backing away. With hate burning in his eyes, Huka lunged after him and caught him around the waist. He lifted him over his head as he would a cattail reed and flung him into the muddy water. Then he turned, snorting and blowing, and charged recklessly at the other beasts.

But this time they turned and ran, quickly disappearing into the reeds.

Now, all was quiet. Mamoot swayed back and forth, blowing and grumbling, rubbing her bleeding chest with the tip of her trunk. Huka waited nearby as a bog turtle poked its head out of the floating moss and scurried across in front of Mamoot. Not far away a bullfrog croaked his deep *Gerr-rummm—Gerr-umm*, and a flock of pintails flew low overhead, their wings whistling in the warm afternoon air.

The old matriarch closed her eyes and hung her head, resting, tired from her futile efforts to pull herself out of her muddy trap.

Then, once again the stillness was shattered by loud hoots and calls as the hunters began a new attack. Mamoot raised her trunk to sniff the air. But this time she picked up another odor, one that she knew well and one she dreaded most of all. It was the smell of fire.

Bleeding profusely from her deep chest wound, she struggled once again to get free. But the thick ooze still held her fast. Then, just over the tops of the swamp reeds she saw the hunters coming back. They had more long sticks and now they held flaming torches high over head.

The old matriarch lifted her head high and rumbled a low vibrating call from deep in her chest. Inaudible to all others, it carried out over the swamps and across the prairie, an infrasonic message to any of her kind within reach. It was an urgent call for help. Then, with anger blazing in her eyes, she turned to face her enemy.

They charged in with their sticks and stones and this time with fire.

Huka was waiting for them. He rushed out to meet them, storming into their midst, flaying at them with his trunk. He knocked two of the beasts to the ground. One got up. The other lay where he fell.

Then Ungog came at him with a flaming torch in one hand and a long stick in the other. He poked the flames in Huka's face, driving him back.

In the meantime other hunters waded in, attacking the old matriarch with sticks and stones.

Mamoot lashed back at them, leaning forward, straining to get at them, but they stayed just out of reach.

In spite of the flaming torches, Huka stormed in again. He charged at Ungog. With a wild swing of his trunk, he knocked the flaming torch out of his hand. It fell into the water and sizzled out.

Ungog dropped his stick and ran off, splashing through the water.

Huka chased after him, then stopped and turned on the other hunters harassing Mamoot. He impaled one on his short tusks and threw him into the water. Then he chased the others through the reeds, keeping them away from the old matriarch.

But Ungog came back, this time with more hunters. They carried blazing torches and waded through the swamp setting the clumps of dry reeds on fire, one at a time, letting the flames spread across the swamp.

Mamoot's eyes grew wide with fright as the yellow fire licked up on all sides. Sparks and hot ashes fell all around her. Desperately she struggled to get free, but her back legs were still mired fast in the bog hole.

The hunters stood just outside the flames throwing stones and sticks. Most of them fell short, but one struck Mamoot on the top of her head and another on her back.

Huka shuddered as a sharp stone struck him on the shoulder, and once again rage burned within him. He splashed through the flames, chasing after the hunters who came too close. Frantically he flayed at the fire, stomping down the burning reeds. But the flames caught on again, sweeping in from every side.

Mamoot was trapped in the center of the blaze. She felt the searing heat and watched the flames creep closer. Caught between the raging fire and the on-slaught of pelting stones, she and Huka were over-whelmed. She stood there now, defenseless, her head down, hunched up against the flying stones.

Huka paced back and forth, beaten and confused, the stench of fire all around him.

Then, in the distance they heard trumpeting and the sound of pounding feet. The ground began to shake.

Ungog and the hunters backed away, their eyes wide with fear. Quickly they threw down their stones and torches and fled the swamp.

The trumpeting grew louder. Mamoot lifted her trunk and trumpeted in answer. Huka ran about in excitement. A moment later Ba and the little family herd came charging into the swamps, their huge bodies splashing through the water, putting out most of the flames.

They gathered at a safe distance around Mamoot. Grunting and grumbling, they reached out and touched her with their trunks.

Then Ba and one of the other cows waded in beside her. They moved quickly to keep from bogging down. They supported her on either side with their shoulders and pushed. The old matriarch leaned forward. Her back legs churned in the loose bog moss. Slowly she began to move ahead. She grunted and strained and little by little she began to climb out. The cows on either side of her pushed harder. She had one foot out of the hole. Then suddenly she slipped and sank all the way back into the bog.

The little herd milled about, rumbling and snorting to each other as if trying to decide what to do.

Once again Ba and one of the other cows plunged

into the patch of ooze and pushed against her shoulders with their heads. Once more Mamoot strained and kicked. With a violent effort she pulled her back legs up under her and started to climb out.

Again she slipped and began to slide back. Huka stood nearby, watching. Suddenly he let out a shrill squeal and splashed into the soft bog moss behind her. He shoved with his head, pushing her forward. Mamoot grunted and groaned, straining mightily. Huka pushed hard, and slowly the old matriarch struggled out of the bog hole.

For a moment Huka was stranded. But he was much lighter, and Ba reached down with her trunk and easily pulled him out.

Tired and bleeding, the old matriarch stood in the shallow water while Ba and the other cows gathered around her, caressing her, touching her with their trunks. She rumbled softly and touched each cow in turn. Then with two cows on either side supporting her, she made her way out of the swamp and onto the prairie. There she lifted her trunk and blasted a trumpeting call of triumph.

The little family waited until dark. Then they traveled slowly, silently, through the darkness toward another swamp, far from this place of violence, where old Mamoot could heal her wounds and live out her days in peace.

17 ▲ THE LAST KILL

FAR OUT ON the plains Equus stood on a low hill watching over his little band of five young mares with their colts and fillies. At six years, he was young, strong and in his prime, a lord of the prairie.

He tossed his head and sniffed the morning breeze. He caught a whiff of an unfamiliar odor, but it was faint and mixed with the scent of the long-horned bison, the camels and the antelopes, and he paid it little heed.

Across the rolling prairie he could see the great herds wandering over the grasslands like swarms of brown beetles. His eyes searched the horizon for signs of prairie lions or dire wolves. He saw none.

But he did see Ungog coming over the rise. Equus watched him closely for a moment, sniffing the air. Now he caught the unfamiliar scent again. It was strong and acrid, but he was not concerned. The strange beast stalked alone through the grass like a tall bird. It made no attempt to creep up or charge, so it was no threat to his mares or colts.

He watched as it came closer. Still he paid little attention. There were always cranes or herons stalking through the grass, hunting for the insects and mice stirred up by the passing herds. This one was larger but no different.

Unconcerned, Equus cantered down the hill and began grazing beside his harem. He lifted his head every few moments and glanced around. He saw a pair of short-tailed grouse fly up as the strange beast came closer.

But he did not see Metan a short distance away, creeping up through the yellow grass, his eyes riveted on one of his dusky colts.

Unaware of the danger, Equus turned back to his grazing. The morning sun warmed his back and he heard the tearing sound as his mares ripped up the stalks of prairie grass.

Then he heard a loud squeal. He spun around to see the dusky colt stumble to the ground, a long stick plunged through his chest.

A moment later Ungog rushed up. He pulled out the spear, then jabbed the colt again and again, ending its life.

For a moment Equus stood there, baffled and uncertain. Then he saw the beast turn toward him and raise the spear. Equus sprang back out of the way, now fully aware that this new beast was dangerous. Without waiting, he galloped through the high grass in a wide circle, rounding up his little band. The colt's mother refused to leave, whinnying softly. Equus nipped at her, driving her away with the others, taking them out of danger.

With hooves pounding, they galloped over the prairie, tails flying out behind them. They raced on until they could no longer smell the frightening odor. When they finally stopped, Equus shook his head and snorted to blow the pungent smell out of his nostrils. Now, like the scent of the saber cats and the lions, it would always be the smell of death.

From his hiding place in the tall grass Metan had seen it all. He had been lying there waiting for his lionesses to make the kill when he saw the strange birdlike creature throw the stick and pin the dusky colt to the ground. He growled deep in his throat, bristling because his prey had been snatched from under his nose. With an angry snarl he sprang up, his tawny body racing across the ground.

Ungog heard him coming as he burst through the dry grass. He shrieked and threw up his hands, his eyes wide with fear. Then he turned and started to run. Metan leaped after him and caught him in full flight. With a wild swing of his great paw he slapped him across the shoulder blades. The impact broke his neck, knocking him to the ground. There he writhed for a moment, then lay still.

Two of Metan's lionesses came out of the tall grass where they had been waiting, ready to pounce. They licked their black lips and sniffed around Ungog's head and neck. Then they curled up their lips and turned away with a snort. They did not like the strange odor.

Metan was already tugging at the body of the dusky colt. He gripped it in his jaws by one of the hind legs, dragging it backward through the grass toward a distant stand of burr oaks. It was almost two years old, large and heavy, and he stopped frequently to rest. The two lionesses followed closely. They sniffed at it but did not try to help. After much tugging and grunting, Metan finally got it into the shade of the trees. There he opened the gut and began to feed. His male hunting companion had wandered off three days ago and had not yet returned. The two females went up into the buckbush thickets to get their cubs and bring them to the kill.

When he had eaten his fill, Metan sauntered farther back into the shade of the trees to sleep and digest his meal. A short while later he was awakened by three well-fed cubs climbing over his head and back. Sleepily he opened his mouth in a wide, gaping yawn. A swarm of blowflies buzzed around his face and he flicked his ears to chase them away.

The three cubs continued to romp around him. One chased the black tuft at the end of his switching tail. The other two chewed on his ears and swatted his face with their small paws. With saintly tolerance, Metan blinked his eyes and let them play.

▴   ▴   ▴

Teratorn soared overhead, following the two-legged hunters. He followed them, as he did the saber cats and the prairie lions, to share in their kills. But these strange creatures stayed around their kills for many days, leaving only a few scattered bones.

This morning he soared beneath the thick puffs of cumulus clouds and watched the drama unfold on the ground below. He saw the hunter kill the dusky colt, and he watched as the lion killed the hunter. He waited while the lion dragged the dead colt off into the trees. Now he circled lower, studying the body of the hunter lying alone and untouched on the open grasslands. He scanned the landscape from horizon to horizon, searching. He saw only the great game herds grazing across the plains. All else seemed quiet. The way was clear.

The warm breeze whispered through his pinions as he swooped down, landing a few feet from the still body. He folded and unfolded his wings like feathery black cloaks. His orange-and-yellow head jerked around as if on a swivel. Satisfied that it was safe, he waddled over to the corpse and hopped up near the shoulder blades, where the neck was broken. Cautiously he leaned down to peck out the eyes. But the eyes and face were pressed flat against the ground. He hopped down and paced awkwardly around the body. He felt uneasy. This carcass was different, the smell was strange. There was little hair, no feathers, no horns or hooves, and there was no tail.

He stood there uncertain, jerking his naked head from side to side, his cold eyes studying the body. Then he heard a faint cry in the distance. He looked up and saw the strange creatures, the hunters he had been following. They came over the hill, running toward him, shouting and waving their sticks.

Quickly Teratorn hopped across the ground. He ran flapping his wings. He caught an updraft coming off the hill. Without the weight of food in his crop he easily swooped into the air. The rising thermal lifted him high. Like a majestic spirit, he sailed out over the prairie. Far below he saw the hunters lift up the dead man and carry him away.

He soared on, following the winding groves of cottonwood trees, the curving riverbanks. He saw the teeming throngs of long-horned bison streaming across the land and the scattered herds of mammoths and horses.

Then, out of the corner of his eye he saw a jackrabbit dashing across the prairie. He folded his wings and plummeted. The rabbit swerved and dodged, but Teratorn swooped after him and plucked him out of the grass.

With the prize dangling from his bill, the great hunting condor sailed for the distant escarpments. There his mate waited with their new chick. The rabbit was a small offering, but Teratorn was not concerned. Tomorrow he would hunt again.

▲ AUTHOR'S NOTE

THROUGH TELEVISION, BOOKS and movies we are, by now, familiar with the great game herds of Africa. The very names Serengeti, Amboseli, and Kilimanjaro conjure up breathtaking vistas of rolling plains filled with immense herds of wildebeests, gazelles, zebras, elephants and rhinos. And lurking in the grass are the predators: the lions, the cheetahs, and leopards. Overhead giant vultures patrol the skies, together with eagles and marabou storks, all searching for a kill, waiting for a meal. It is a scene directly out of the prehistoric, the late Pleistocene.

What is not so well known is that North America's Pleistocene age once rivaled Africa's for its spectacular scenery and teeming wildlife. The American prairie lions were magnificent beasts, long-legged and swift but without the heavily maned head and shoulders of their African counterparts. For thousands of years they roamed the midwestern plains in small groups, dominating territories and sometimes following the wandering bison.

Vast herds of elk, mammoths and mastodons literally covered the plains from Manitoba to Texas. Lithe, long-limbed camels intermingled with three species of antelopes, one no larger than a jack rabbit.

This book is an attempt to portray the beauty and majesty of that forgotten late Pleistocene age. Yet it is far from complete. Because of space limitations and the demands of story, many of the animals and birds that existed at that time—American zebras, giant short-faced bears, cheetahs and armored glyptodonts—are not mentioned.

It was a marvelous world of giants, second only to the age of dinosaurs. Hopefully, this book will be able to reveal a small hint of that colorful past.